# Here's what readers are saying about The Traveling Tea Ladies!

"As owner of The Tea Academy and Miss Melanie's Tea Room & Gourmet Tea Emporium, Melanie O'Hara has made a seamless foray into murder and mayhem set among tea enthusiasts in the South. Her primary women characters, Amelia, Olivia, Cassandra and Sarah, combine sophistication with compassion and eccentricity as they drink tea in Amelia's Victorian tea room, experiment with delectable recipes and juggle jobs, family, social calendars and shopping. Their trip from the sleepy town of Dogwood Cove, Tennessee, to the big city of Dallas for a girl's weekend exceeds their expectations for "adventure" when murder is unexpectedly added to the menu. In the tradition of the British cozy mystery, *The Traveling Tea Ladies* blends quirky characters, good food and drink with mystery and intrigue."

Judy Slagle, Department Chair of Literature and Languages
East Tennessee State Unviersity

"Melanie O'Hara opens the door on unexpected intrigue from the genteel tea rooms of East Tennessee. The mystery is steeped in local color as the tea ladies muster their forces to help a friend in need. Readers will want to put a pot on and do some traveling themselves."

Randall Brown, Writer, *Knoxville News Sentinel*

"Talk about a perfect book to read at the beach … entertaining and intriguing! Melanie O'Hara is a young woman whose background of owning a tea room has provided the perfect experiences for her unique books about *The Traveling Tea Ladies!*

*The Traveling Tea Ladies: Death in Dixie* is a story that shows the deep friendships and loyalty of four friends who share an acute interest in tea. I found myself making notes of certain types of tea to try and could almost taste some of the tea foods and candy the author described.

This second book of Melanie's does make you wonder what can happen to these creative and resourceful women next. I can't wait—the next book will take place in Savannah!"

Kathy Knight
Accent Editor, *The Greeneville Sun*

"I guarantee that once you start this book, you will not be able to put it down. In fact, I was so connected to the storyline that I almost missed my train stop. Rarely do I find a book that can capture my attention so deeply that I forget I am riding to work on the noisy NYC subway. I highly recommend this book. It's perfect for a book club or to give your best friend as a gift. Every time I sat down to read this book, I felt I was getting together with my closest friends. It is a true gem indeed. I cannot wait to read about the next adventure The Traveling Tea Ladies take on."

Patty Aizaga, NYCGirlAtHeart.com

## Other titles in
## The Traveling Tea Ladies series

The Traveling Tea Ladies
*Death in Dallas*

The Traveling Tea Ladies
*Death in Dixie*

The Traveling Tea Ladies
*Death in the Low Country*

The Traveling Tea Ladies
*Till Death Do Us Part*

## Other books by Melanie O'Hara

Savannah Skies
*Return to Tybee Island*

Savannah Skies
*Changing Tides*

Melanie O'Hara

# THE TRAVELING TEA LADIES

## Viva Las Vegas

LYONS
LEGACY
PUBLISHING™

Johnson City, Tennessee

The Traveling Tea Ladies™
*Viva Las Vegas*
Copyright © 2013 Melanie O'Hara
All rights reserved.

Cover art by Susi Galloway
www.SusiGalloway.com

Book design by Longfeather Book Design
www.LongfeatherBookDesign.com

LYONS
LEGACY
PUBLISHING™

You may contact the publisher at:
Lyons Legacy Publishing™
123 East Unaka Aveneue
Johnson City, Tennessee 37601
Publisher@LyonsLegacyPublishing.com

ISBN: 978-0-9836145-2-4 (paperback)
ISBN: 978-0-9836145-6-2 (ebook)

*For my friends, the readers who have joined me on this tea adventure. Your support and kind words have provided endless inspiration for the series. From the bottom of my heart I thank you!*

# Acknowledgements

"It takes a village …" and I'm lucky to have a very supportive village.

A heart felt thank you once again to Phyllis Estepp for her sharp editing skills! You're quite a remarkable lady and I appreciate you.

A big shout out to the creative team at Longfeather Book Design. Without you, "the ladies" would be rather ordinary. Thank you for your meticulous attention to detail and your positive attitude. I've so enjoyed working with you over the years.

Bravo to Susi Galloway and her artistry. The Tea Ladies have never looked better!

Lastly thank you to my husband Keith (the real-life Shane Spencer) and my children. I'd never have the courage to write without your love and encouragement. I'm blessed beyond measure.

# THE TRAVELING TEA LADIES

## Viva Las Vegas

# CHAPTER ONE

"*I*'m worried about her, Amelia. Has she returned your phone calls lately?" Olivia asked as she took another sip of her tea and devoured the last few bites of bluegrass derby pie. "You've outdone yourself today, Lily. Would you box two of these pies to go? Lincoln will go ape over this dessert!"

I had to shake my head and chuckle to myself. No matter what the circumstances, food was always at the forefront with Olivia Lincoln, formerly Olivia Rivers and Dogwood Cove's most recent newlywed.

"Two pies to go coming right up," Lily smiled and turned to fill the order. I was overjoyed her bakery was doing a brisk business despite nationwide economic troubles. Keeping a small business afloat was never easy, but with homemade confections like Lily's, it was hard to resist stopping in for a fresh baked treat.

"Seriously, Amelia, I haven't heard from her all week. It's not like her to not check in with me at least once a day."

"I haven't heard from Cassandra either. I was hoping you had. That's why I wanted you to meet me. I'm trying to respect her privacy, but I'm worried about her, Liv. She looked so thin the last time I saw her at the Dogwood Cove Symphony Showcase house," I recalled as I wiped the traces of cherry cream cheese brownie from the corners of my mouth.

"She's made it crystal clear to me she doesn't want to discuss Doug. Why is she so insistent on protecting that scumbag? I would've sold my story to *The National Enquirer* by now," the redhead spitfire declared as she set down her fork with a clang.

"Keep your voice down, Liv!" I implored. We live in a very small tight-knit community. Bad news travels lightning fast in Dogwood Cove like a tricked-out muscle car with nitrogen boosters. "This is precisely why she doesn't share every intimate detail with you because you get too angry and she doesn't need that right now." I scanned the dining room to be certain the other patrons weren't eavesdropping.

"Maybe Cassandra hasn't decided what to do yet. Have you considered the possibility she may reconcile with Doug? They may work it out."

"Work it out? Have you totally lost your marbles, Amelia? After what he did with Dixie and who knows how many other women, how could she ever forgive him?" Olivia argued.

She had a point. It had been humiliating for Cassandra to find out that her long-time event planner had been having an affair with her husband. Cassandra and Doug had been married for over ten years and had made the difficult decision not to have children because of her position as CEO of *his* family's third generation business. She'd been supportive while he ran for the Tennessee House of Representatives and managed Reynolds's Candies on her own while he lived in Nashville. But I had to keep reminding myself that every marriage is different. I didn't know if they'd move past this, but if Hillary forgave Bill, Cassandra might excuse Doug.

"Maybe that's why she hasn't been telling us everything. They could be going to counseling. If there's any shred of hope for reconciliation, she wouldn't trash talk Doug to her closest friends," I reasoned.

We were momentarily interrupted when Lily brought two bubblegum pink bakery boxes over to our table. "I'll take care of this at the register when you're ready. Can I get you another pot of jasmine tea, ladies?"

"Are you ready to leave or do we have time for another pot?" Olivia asked me.

"I'm in no hurry," I reassured her. "I think another pot would be great. Thanks Lily!"

Lily's Bakery was one of the businesses in Dogwood Cove that carried our company's gourmet loose teas and organic coffees. Starting Smoky Mountain Coffee, Herb and Tea Company with my husband, Shane Spencer, had been a wise decision. I had recently sold my tea room to good friend Sarah McCaffrey in order to spend more time with my family and manage our booming wholesale business. We had to expand our warehouse staff to ten full-time employees to keep ahead of the Internet orders.

One of the perks of setting my own schedule was time to stop for a pot of tea or lunch with a friend. When I owned the Pink Dogwood Tea Room, I rarely had time to take a few bites of food before the next big reservation arrived. I did miss the day-to-day interaction with the guests and the ambiance of the beautiful Victorian tea house but I didn't miss the four AM mornings to bake scones and prepare the tea tray goodies. Sarah was learning the ropes of the tea room business and so far seemed to be enjoying the rush.

"Any chance you might be available for a tea tasting if I get a group together? We have a number of book clubs and knitting groups that meet here. A few members expressed an interest in learning more about tea," Lily said.

"I think we can arrange it as long as it is not during World Tea Expo next month." I had so much to do to get our booth ready. This would be the first year Smoky Mountain would participate as a vendor. I'd been to World Tea Expo countless times and had enjoyed the educational seminars hosted by the leaders in the tea industry. This year would be a vastly different experience. It was challenging to predict how many coffees and teas we would need for sampling. There were endless details to plan for the three-day event.

"World Tea Expo? There's actually an expo just for tea?" Lily asked surprised.

"I get that reaction a lot," I agreed. "Tea is the second most consumed beverage in the world just slightly behind water. It's an eight billion dollar industry in the US alone. The general public doesn't realize how quickly tea is growing in popularity. Did you know Starbucks just acquired Teavana for six hundred twenty million dollars last year?"

"I had no idea tea was such a 'hot' commodity, pun intended," Lily joked. "Your jasmine tea is almost ready. I'll be right back."

"Speaking of World Tea Expo," Olivia interjected, "is Cassandra still going?"

"As far as I know she was the last time we spoke. Reynolds's Candies is promoting their tea truffles at the event. Our booth is next to Cassandra's."

I'd spent time in Paris with Cassandra and the chefs at Reynolds's headquarters developing a line of tea-infused truffles. Not only were these wonderful candies rich in taste, they were full of antioxidants and polyphenols from the tea that was masterfully blended with different varieties of chocolate. The orange blossom oolong with dark chocolate and the genmaicha green tea with milk chocolate were among my favorites.

"Do you think she'll go? Las Vegas might not be her idea of fun with everything she's going through right now," Olivia said with concern in her voice. She adjusted the emerald engagement ring on her left hand and continued. "I can't imagine what I'd do if Lincoln betrayed me. I think I'd take a pitchfork to him!" she half-way joked as she twisted her ring and looked up wistfully. I've noticed when one of your friends receives bad news, it's natural to take a step back and re-evaluate your own life and relationships.

"I don't think you've anything to worry about, Liv. Matt Lincoln adores you. I've never seen a man more smitten. You're lucky," I reassured her and patted her hand.

I was confident Olivia and Matt had a solid marriage. Their wedding held at Riverbend Ranch seven months ago continued to be the talk of the town. They seemed relaxed and blissfully happy together.

In the past I'd been concerned Olivia wouldn't find

someone who could stand toe-to-toe with her. She was proudly independent and ran her therapeutic horseback riding center almost singlehandedly. She was a mere five feet tall, but one day of ranch work proved she could out rope, out bale and out work most men. Detective Matt Lincoln was the right guy to tame our wild filly. He'd moved from Dallas and joined our police force.

"We planned on going together. It won't be the same without Cassandra," Olivia said tearfully. The two polar opposites were the best of friends. Cassandra who was a regular on Dogwood Cove's "Top Ten Best Dressed" list had taken Wrangler wearing cowgirl Olivia under her wing and introduced her to the world of fashion. She'd even convinced Olivia to attend Fashion Week in New York and helped her discover her inner "fashion diva."

"Sarah will be there purchasing teas and giftware for the tea room. And Aunt Imogene has decided to tag along with Lucy. Those two will make the trip worthwhile," I chortled at the thought of my favorite leopard wearing aunt and her roommate making the trip to "Sin City." Imogene was young at heart and wore four-inch stilettos despite her advancing age. She claimed in her youth she'd been involved with Wayne Newton. It wouldn't surprise me with all the beaus she'd had over the years.

"I love your aunt and her brashness. She says whatever's on her mind."

"There's a saying in my family that Imogene's missing a filter between her brain and her mouth. She thinks it and so she says it with brutal honesty. I admit I sometimes cringe when she arrives at gatherings. I love her to pieces, but you never know what she might say," I told her.

"Do you follow her Twitter or Facebook page? She says the most outrageous things. She's worse than Joan Rivers on *The Fashion Police,*" Olivia scoffed and peered inside the box. "Gosh that pie smells incredible. I'm thinking of having another slice," she said as she eyed the rich chocolate bourbon pie.

"I've known you for years and I still don't know how you do it!" I remarked. "How can you eat more than anyone I know and stay so thin?"

"High metabolisms run in my family," Olivia explained as she carefully cut another healthy slice of pie, "plus the chores I do around the farm. I'm constantly moving, working with the horses, the cattle, the kids. I'm exhausted by the time I go to sleep at night. Want a slice?" she offered.

"No thank you, I'd better not this close to dinner. We'll have a good time regardless of whether Cassandra goes or not, but I do hope she's coming," I said returning to the more serious side of our conversation. "Shane has tried to reach out to Doug several times and he's always told by his administrative assistant he's in a meeting or on another call. Doug's been extremely elusive."

"He knows better than to speak to me," Olivia warned. "I can't stand cheaters. When I heard he'd been running around with *my* wedding planner, I wanted to tie him to a tree in the middle of a field, douse him with BBQ sauce and leave him to the critters. He's a poor excuse for a man!" she vented.

"You paint a vivid picture, Liv!" I laughed at the thought of preppy, proper Doug Reynolds being tied to a tree covered in BBQ sauce. No, it wasn't a nice thought, but it's what he deserved. Cassandra didn't deserve this type of embarrassment.

"Well friend, have we solved all the world's problems today?" I joked.

"Speaking of a problem don't look now but one just walked through the door," Olivia warned as I looked over my shoulder at the jingling of the front door bell. Oh, dear! It was Sally Stokes, my former realtor and the town's neb-nose. Dealing with her reminded me of fingernails scratching a chalkboard.

"Hi y'all!" Sally called out and flapped her arms like a duck. Her ample hips swayed slowly back and forth in her tight orange tweed suit. She made a bee line to our table.

"Hi, Sally. Beautiful weather today," I smiled, attempting to make polite small talk as I inwardly cringed.

"Sally," Olivia said curtly. She continued eating her pie and looked down at her plate trying her best to ignore her.

"Isn't it just awful about Cassandra and Doug?" Sally exclaimed dramatically placing her hand over her heart. "Did either of you have any idea he was having an affair with that Beverly Hills vixen?" she pried.

"Why would you ask us about Cassandra and Doug?" I challenged her.

"Well, I know how close y'all are and I'm assuming when they divorce, you might put in a good word for me when the assets need to be divided," she said with a saccharin grin pasted on her pale face.

Was she really so callous and calculating that she would cross the line and ask something so tacky and reprehensible? Oh the nerve of this woman! Every time Sally was around, she managed to be offensive and got my blood boiling. Today took the cake. She had sunk to an all-time low.

"Sally, I don't know the source of your information, but you've been misinformed," I said firmly hoping to shut her up. "I'm not aware of Cassandra and Doug filing for divorce."

"What assets are you referring to?" Olivia demanded giving Sally her full attention. "Quit beating around the bush, Sally. I hope you're not planning on doing something as vulgar as approaching Cassandra on selling her house?"

"The thought has crossed my mind. A couple with that much wealth will have to divide properties when they go their separate ways. There's the home in Palm Beach, the villa in Paris, the home in Sonoma Valley and the lake house here in Tennessee," she said as she began counting properties on her swollen sausage-like fingers. "We're talking about a hefty commission to the broker who sells those. I was thinking if you'd put a good word in for me…"

"Let me tell you what I'll do for you, Sally!" Olivia exploded as she abruptly stood up from the table.

"Liv, Liv. Settle down," I warned pulling her arm to get her to sit back down. "Sally, we're not going to discuss Cassandra's personal life. If you're that interested in listing her properties, contact her yourself."

"I just thought … oh never mind! Amelia, tell your handsome husband hello. You girls have a nice day. Tootles!" she called out as she quickly moved over to the bakery display.

"Ugh, that woman irks me!" Olivia seethed. "Of all the nerve, asking us to put in a good word! I can't believe her!"

"Some people are tasteless and never change. She

almost ruined the deal when we were buying the tea room," I recollected.

"She's a vulture," Olivia shuddered as she continued eating her pie. "Oh good, here's our tea. Thank you Lily," Olivia beamed as she refilled our tea cups. We tried our best to ignore Sally moving from table to table gossiping with the patrons.

"I'm assuming Lucy has been to World Tea Expo since she owned Lyla's Tea Room?" Olivia asked referring to Aunt Imogene's roommate. She'd turned over the reins to her niece Darla and officially retired from the day-to-day running of the well-known establishment in neighboring Jonesborough. Lucy remained actively involved in the business and enjoyed going to the Atlanta Gift Market and World Tea Expo to purchase items for Lyla's.

"She's been countless times over the years. Lucy knows everyone in the tea business. She's practically a walking tea encyclopedia," I said and sipped my tea. I felt my shoulders begin to relax after Sally's invasion. I wished she'd hurry up and leave instead of continuing to be so loud and obtrusive.

"Matt's doesn't fully understand the whole tea thing or the North American Tea Championship, but he's hoping to play golf and go to the casinos with Shane," Olivia said.

"I'm sure Shane will need time to relax once the expo is over. Don't remind me about the tea championships or my stomach will be tied in knots again," I smiled and placed my hands across my abdomen.

I was nervous about our first year competing with such a distinguished group of tea producers. The competition awarded winners in several categories for best tasting and highest quality teas in North America. I didn't know the outcome, but I knew it would be a good experience for our business. We were competing in both the hot tea and iced tea groups this year.

"Amelia, I don't know how you manage a family and a business. My hat's off to you," Olivia said. "I'm still trying to get used to this whole married thing and remain balanced. It's not easy for us to spend time together between ranch chores, riding lessons, and his police schedule. I wouldn't be able to manage everything if we had kids right now."

"Are you thinking of starting a family?" I inquired since she had broached the subject. Olivia had waited a long time to meet her "Mr. Right". Over the years she had helped many emotionally and physically challenged children through therapeutic horseback riding lessons at Riverbend Ranch. I had no doubts she'd be a wonderful mother.

"We've talked about it and dreamed about it, but I don't know if it's realistic for us right now. He says he's ready, but I think it would be best to wait a while."

"No matter how much you pre-plan and try to choose the perfect time, most parents would say there isn't a perfect time. Sometimes you have trust it will all work out," I smiled as I remembered when Shane and I first started planning our family. Emma was our first born and now had her learner's permit to drive. Time had certainly flown by!

"Did you worry having children would change everything?" Olivia asked in earnest. "All the sudden the baby's the center of everything," Olivia explained. "You're no longer just a couple. You're a family. And sometimes couples can drift apart. I don't want that to happen. I know it sounds self-centered, but I'd like my husband to myself a little longer before we have kids. Matt doesn't feel the same way. He's ready to start now."

"Your wedding was this past October. You're still in the honeymoon phase. You two have plenty of time to start a family. Have you told him how you feel?"

"I've tried several times and he doesn't understand. Family's everything to him. He had a great childhood and he and his brother Tom are close. I can't say I share his sentiments regarding family," Olivia sadly said as she stirred her teaspoon and adjusted her napkin.

I had a feeling I knew what she was worrying about. Olivia had a somewhat contentious relationship with her mother, Ruby Rivers. In fact, Ruby had nearly ruined Olivia's wedding. The two were working on mending fences, but I assumed Olivia was concerned history would be repeated.

"You and Ruby are doing better, Liv. Not everyone has the ideal family. You don't have to continue the same patterns when you have children," I quietly reminded her.

"I miss my Dad so much, Amelia. It was always the two of us. My mother was jealous and lashed out constantly. I know you don't believe me, but I had a difficult childhood."

"Oh, I believe you, Liv! I was at your bridal shower, remember?" I teased. "Your mom is one-of-a-kind. I'm relieved she didn't ruin your wedding day."

"Sarah and Grandma Laurel helped me to see things straight when Mama acted poorly. Speaking of Sarah, where is she? I thought she would be here by now," Olivia observed glancing at her watch.

"She's probably had a late reservation," I assumed. "The tea room is such a lovely setting, guests can't help but linger." I looked over my shoulder toward the front door of the bakery to watch for the arrival of the third lady in our tea foursome. We were known about town as "The Traveling Tea Ladies" and had earned the nickname from our frequent travels and penchant for mayhem.

"There she is," I smiled broadly and waved as Sarah briskly came through the door.

"Sorry I'm late! I got caught up with a group of Red Hat Ladies who were buying everything in sight. I didn't realize the time!" she explained blowing her brunette bangs out of the way. She adjusted her red-rimmed Sally Jesse Raphael style glasses and took a seat.

"Don't worry, Sarah, I completely understand. I hope you had good sales," I said.

"We did. We did. They all send their best, Amelia. It was the 'Red Hot Mamas' from Elizabethton. They're so sweet," she said and glanced over at the bakery display. "I've probably held you up, so I won't order anything."

"Don't be silly, Sarah. Get a pot of tea or share our Jasmine. I'm in no hurry today. Shane's picking up Charlie from football and Emma is at choir practice. There's a roast in the oven, so I can take my time getting home."

"What's good today? You know, I feel like a cup of homemade Italian meatball soup. Anyone else care to join me?" Sarah proposed.

Lily had recently added a light lunch menu to her baked items to increase business. Each day she had two made-from-scratch soups and a sandwich special. The new fare had gone over well with the Main Street shoppers and business crowd.

"That sounds like a plan," Olivia agreed. I shook my head in amusement. Of course she would join Sarah for soup. Sarah walked over to the counter and placed an order for two cups of the delicious soup laden with tomatoes, Italian green beans, kidney beans, and of course homemade mini meatballs and a pot of blackberry bramble tea.

"What? What's so funny?" Olivia asked defensively.

"Nothing, nothing at all! So, Sarah," I said changing the subject, "catch us up with what you've been doing."

"We've had so many reservations for graduation, bridal showers and teacher appreciation tea parties. If I didn't live above the tea room I'd never get home!" she exclaimed.

"It's high season for you. Not quite as busy as fall and Christmas, but almost. Are you sure you can get away for World Tea Expo this year? It sounds like you're covered up," I worried.

"I'm not missing my first World Tea Expo, no way, no how! I've called in the troops to man the 'Pink Lady' while I'm away. Gretchen's been doing an excellent job as manager. I'm looking forward to this trip especially with everything going on with Cassandra," she insisted.

"Have you heard from her?" Olivia asked as the soup was placed in front of her. She grabbed her spoon not waiting for Sarah's reply before diving into the bowl.

"I saw her last week. She came to the tea room for lunch with Thomas Simpson," she disclosed.

"Thomas Simpson, her attorney?" Olivia squawked nearly spitting her soup out. "What was *he* doing there?"

"I didn't ask," Sarah said as she placed her napkin in her lap. "They requested a private table and I gave them space on the porch by themselves."

"You didn't think to ask? I can't believe it!" Olivia said incredulously.

"Liv, I pride myself on not poking into other people's affairs. Discretion is vital these days. Between the celebrity gossip and advances in technology, I think people constantly cross the line. What should be private and what should be public? I don't need to know every detail of a friend's day on Facebook. 'I washed the dog. Now I'm doing laundry. Now I'm frying an egg.' It's just ridiculous!"

"I have to admit, I like my celebrity gossip and Amelia's Aunt Imogene does Tweet hilarious comments. But I'm worried about Cassandra. She's my closest and dearest friend and she's practically shut me out of her life. I want to help, but I don't know what's going on," Olivia said sounding exasperated.

"Thomas Simpson is the attorney for Reynolds's Candies. It could have been a business meeting, Liv. Let's not jump to conclusions," I cautioned.

"Point taken, but they may have been discussing the division of the company or if Cassandra will keep her current position should they divorce. This is a complicated situation because she's running his family's business. She's the heart and soul of Reynolds's. If it weren't for her Hollywood connections, Reynolds's Candies wouldn't have been in the gift bags at the Oscars. She's put an old and established business back on the map by marketing the heck out of it and developing new trends in the chocolate world. Doug should be kissing her feet. Instead he took a beautiful partnership and flushed it down toilet," Olivia reflected.

"I couldn't agree with you more. All we can do is let Cassandra have her space and be there for her in whatever capacity she allows us," Sarah said quietly.

"Eventually we'll know. The trip is coming up and she offered to fly us out. I'll call her and ask if she still plans on going. We may need to book tickets if she's changed her mind," I thought aloud.

"Not a problem. I'll call Mandy at Dogwood Travel and see what's available in case we need a backup plan," Sarah offered.

"And I'll calm down, I promise!" Olivia said as she took the last bite of soup. "I'll have to start thinking of what to pack. I've never been to Vegas so I don't know what to expect."

"Wear something flashy and outrageous! I am," Sarah disclosed.

"Oh good gravy, I can only imagine some of the getups you are planning on wearing," Olivia chuckled.

"Getups? What do you mean?" Sarah asked innocuously.

"No offense intended, Sarah, but you always wear something edgy. I don't feel comfortable taking fashion risks," Olivia clarified.

"You mean the sari I wore to the cocktail party in Dallas?" Sarah questioned.

"You did look beautiful in that outfit Sarah," I spoke up trying to diffuse a potentially delicate situation. "Olivia is more about Wrangler jeans and boots. You know she's far more practical with her fashion choices."

"I was thinking of your hardhat with spelunking headlamp, your EMF meter and messenger bag full of your *Ghost Busters* paraphernalia. I could have died when you flipped on your headlamp beam during the ghost walk tour in Jonesborough," Olivia chuckled.

"Let's not bring that up again," I warned the girls. Sarah was very touchy about her beliefs in ghosts and the supernatural. Olivia was walking through a potential mine field.

"Olivia you're still questioning whether or not ghosts exist? I thought with everything that occurred, you of all people would've changed your mind," Sarah said sensitively.

"I don't believe in that paranormal nonsense. You dragged me to so many haunted landmarks in Savannah, I lost count. If I'd walked into one more haunted home or hotel, I think my feet would've fallen off," Olivia joked.

"Think what you want. One of the reasons I'm excited about going to Las Vegas is one of my favorite authors will be at Comic Con that same weekend.

"Comic Con? What the heck?" Olivia wondered aloud.

"Comic Con is the largest comic book convention in the world. Everyone in the sci-fi industry attends Comic Con," Sarah patiently explained.

"Like who?" Olivia challenged. "I've never heard of it."

"For one, Robert Downy, Jr. because he was *Iron Man*, Rob Pattinson from *Twilight*…"

"Oh I know what you're talking about," Olivia interrupted. "That's the conventions for all the sci-fi geeks who dress up like their favorite characters from *Star Wars* and *Star Trek*."

"I'm going to ignore your rude remarks. You only said that because I dressed up like Princess Leia for your costume party. You have such a small mind, Olivia!" she said as she crossed her arms and looked away.

"I say what I think. I'm sorry if that hurt your feelings," Olivia quipped.

"Ok, that's enough, you two. Liv, you need to work on your 'filter' or people will talk about you like they do Aunt Imogene. I'm listening, Sarah. You never did tell us about your favorite author. Who is he? Have I heard of him?" I intervened.

"Jonathan Kirk, the author of the series, *A Ghost's Guide to Understanding the Modern World*. I've read every one of his books at least three times."

"*A Ghost's Guide to Understanding the Modern World*? I'm a bit confused. I wasn't aware ghosts read books," Olivia guffawed.

"His book gives the reader a perspective into how a ghost views our world. It helps the layman realize the confusion of being caught between two dimensions. Quoting Professor Kirk, 'when we can empathize with their plight, we can co-exist and help them find the light.'"

"Sarah, I don't know what's in your well water, but you can't seriously believe this nonsense," Olivia pronounced.

"If you bothered to read one of his books, you'd understand. Ghosts are not ghouls or demons. They were at one time honorable citizens and townspeople who are trying to complete unfinished business. They need our help," she concluded.

"Help a ghost? First of all, I don't believe they exist and

secondly if they did exist, I wouldn't take the time to explain to the ghost why it was living between two dimensions. I'd run to the hills as fast as I could," Olivia declared.

"I knew you wouldn't understand. If you're blocked and negative, you can't be open to thinking beyond our world," Sarah said obviously frustrated.

"Let's agree to disagree on this subject," I suggested. I cleared my throat and nudged Olivia under the table. On more than one occasion when the subject of ghosts had arisen these two had nearly come to blows. Sarah was very gullible and naïve while Olivia was a true skeptic. They were good friends but didn't always see eye-to-eye.

"I'm going to get Jonathan Kirk's autograph and picture. It would be a dream come true for me," Sarah babbled.

"More like a nightmare in my opinion," Olivia murmured to herself.

"I dare you to come with me, Liv. Meet him for yourself. He's giving a lecture during Comic Con on the supernatural. Why don't you come?" Sarah challenged her.

"You wouldn't catch me dead at that circus side show," Olivia said rebelliously and crossed her arms.

"I didn't think you would. You're afraid to confront your deepest fears," Sarah speculated and took another spoonful of her soup.

"What fears? I'm not afraid of anything," Olivia laughed and leaned across the table towards Sarah.

"You claim ghosts don't exist, but you make too many sarcastic remarks. I think maybe you had an encounter with an apparition during your childhood and ever since, you have distanced yourself from discussing anything to do with the supernatural," Sarah concluded knowingly.

"See, that's what's wrong with you Sarah. You research topics to the umpteenth degree and then you try to transfer your feelings onto other people. I hate to burst your bubble, *Miss Marple*, but I'm not a believer on any level, conscious or subconscious and I've never had an encounter with a spirit, ghost, goblin or ghoul. I'm a doubting Thomas when it comes to believing that beings caught between dimensions roam the earth and cause trouble. Sarah you need to get a new hobby. I've allowed you to drag me to every haunted hotel, inn, restaurant, and graveyard in Savannah, but I draw the line at attending a lecture by this Kirk Johns guy," Olivia concluded.

"His name is Jonathan Kirk," Sarah said deflated. I knew she was touchy after Olivia's upbraiding.

"If I have time, I'll go with you," I volunteered.

"You would? That would be fantastic!" Sarah acknowledged as her spirits lifted.

"You've lost it Amelia. You don't realize you opened up a can of worms," Olivia whispered in warning in my ear. "Are you trying to make me look bad?"

"I think it sounds like fun. I've never been to Comic Con. I might enjoy rubbing elbows with Luke Skywalker and the Hulk," I joked trying to settle the disagreement between my two girlfriends.

"I'll see if I can reserve seats. I'm sure a lecture with Jonathan Kirk will sell out. After all, he's the foremost authority in the supernatural," Sarah claimed excitedly.

"And the foremost authority in nut jobs," Olivia muttered. I shot her a dirty look that pleaded for her to behave.

"Speaking of reserved seats, I'd better get home. I'm sure a hungry crew's waiting on me," I said looking at my watch. "If either of you hear from Cassandra, have her call me," I requested.

"You've got it Amelia," Sarah promised.

"I've got a handsome husband who will do just about anything for a slice of this pie," Olivia announced as she rose from the table and pushed in her chair. She adjusted her long curls and lifted the bakery boxes by the string.

"Anything?" Sarah sniggered and put her hand over her mouth. I was satisfied she wasn't upset with Olivia. I wanted our trip to Las Vegas to go as smooth as possible.

"You'd be surprised what a man will do for a little dessert," Olivia grinned and raised her eyebrows provocatively.

"On that note, I'm leaving," I giggled and hugged each of them goodbye.

# CHAPTER TWO

"Should I wait for Cassandra to call or just take the plunge and call her myself?" I asked Shane as we sat around the kitchen table enjoying a soothing cup of white peony tea and reviewing the day's events.

"World Tea Expo is a business event for Reynolds's Candies as well as Smoky Mountain Coffee, Herb and Tea Company. You've got to put your business hat on to handle this situation," he advised.

"You understand my dilemma. I don't want to be perceived as being pushy but she needs her privacy right now." I inhaled the aroma of the tea as I tried to think things out. Cassandra was not acting like herself and I felt off balance in dealing with the trip to Vegas.

"She offered to take the corporate jet and fly us as well as our booth display and inventory out to Las Vegas for the weekend. If we make alternative plans to ship our equipment or haul it to Nevada ourselves, we should figure this out now. Please quit beating around the bush and call her," Shane said emphatically. "If she doesn't plan on attending, we'll still go. We have too much riding on the North American Tea Championship this year."

He was right. Placing in the North American Tea Championship would help our company break out within the tea industry and dramatically impact our sales. In the past, a fourth or even third place award to a company had garnered attention. I needed to stay focused on our business goals and the importance of competing this year.

"I'll call her in the morning and ask if she's going," I agreed.

"It's not late, Amelia. Call her now under the assumption she's attending. You'll sleep better once you know her decision and I'll sleep better knowing if I need to start making alternate plans. I'm not sure I can handle a drive to Nevada with your Aunt Imogene and Lucy in tow," he grinned and rubbed my arm for assurance.

"You're right. I'll call her now," I said and rose from the table to grab the phone. I punched in her number and waited uneasily for her to answer.

"Cassandra Reynolds," she brusquely answered on the third ring.

"Cassandra, it's Amelia," I said nervously. "Just checking on the trip to Vegas," I said awkwardly. "Is everything still on track?" I asked as I held my breath and looked over at Shane who was leaning across the table.

"Of course! I wouldn't miss it for the 'world!'" she joked and a wave of relief washed over me.

"Great! I was hoping you'd say that. We're all looking forward to the weekend, especially Aunt Imogene. She claims she had a relationship with Wayne Newton back in the day and she's determined to track him down," I tittered.

"I'm sorry to cut this short, Amelia, but I'm meeting with Thomas Simpson in a few minutes and I think I heard him pull up. Let's get together soon and have lunch at the Pink Dogwood, OK?" she hastily said as I heard a click and the phone disconnect.

"That was odd," I said aloud as I looked at the phone in confusion. Had she really abruptly hung up without saying goodbye? That was not like her at all. In the south, we pride ourselves on our manners and we're raised to be congenial even towards unwanted pesky sales calls.

"She's still going," Shane stated. "You and Liv have worried yourselves to death about it. It's best to go directly to the source and deal with the facts," he said smugly, rather proud of himself that he had easily solved yet another problem.

"She practically hung up on me," I told him shaking my head in disbelief. "She's acting oddly. One second everything is fine, let's have lunch and then she has to go because Thomas Simpson pulled up."

"Amelia, don't read too much into that," he warned.

"I'm trying not to, but she's been seen around town with him and now he's coming over to her house in the evening. There must be some major legal deliberations going on."

"And it's none of our business. She'll share everything when she's ready," he lectured.

"I've been friends with Cassandra for years. Even Olivia doesn't know what's going on. She's been avoiding her too and they're best friends," I shared with him.

"Everyone is different when they have marital issues.

Some people want to discuss it with everyone in the world from their barber to their grocery cashier. Other people are more private and keep things close to the vest. Cassandra has been under a microscope since Doug threw his hat into the political arena. I'm sure she's been advised to keep this under wraps," Shane concluded.

"I've never had to be careful with what I've said to any of my friends. I feel like I have to walk on eggshells with her."

"She may feel the same way," Shane said turning the tables. "What if she's been told she's not allowed to discuss Doug as part of some contractual agreement between their attorneys? That places her in a very isolated position. She wouldn't be able to turn to her friends for support. She'll find herself at the mercy of the press when this does become public and it will, Amelia," he predicted. "Doug Reynolds has been rumored to be a candidate for Governor of Tennessee. A scandalous affair could ruin his chances of being elected."

"I was telling Olivia there's always the possibility they're trying to work things out. What if Doug comes to Las Vegas with Cassandra?" I suddenly thought out loud. "I can't speak for everyone else, but I would feel extremely uncomfortable if he did decide to tag along," I said with an apprehensive tone in my voice.

Attempting to steady my nerves Shane said, "Let's focus on the North American Tea Championship and making sure we pack everything we need for our booth. We can't sit around wringing our hands about Doug and Cassandra. She's a big girl, Amelia. She'll handle it."

"What would I say to him if he showed up? I haven't seen him since the affair with Dixie was exposed. 'Hi Doug, so nice for you to stab my good friend in the back and humiliate her when she's been so loyal to you and your family business,'" I said sarcastically whipping my hands in the air for dramatic emphasis.

"Amelia, most likely Doug isn't coming. He has business in Nashville. Right now a trip to Vegas might be perceived as frivolous when he's attempting to raise votes and money for his run as governor. How many business trips have we gone on and Cassandra traveled solo?" he reminded me.

"You're right. Doug has been MIA for many of Reynolds's events. I can't remember the last time the four of us had dinner together. I don't know why I'm so bothered by this," I said as I grabbed a towel and began vigorously cleaning the granite countertops. Chores around the house are a good diversion when I have much on my mind.

"I'll have to have the granite re-sealed if you keep rubbing it like that," Shane joked and took the towel from me. "Why don't you let me run a bubble bath for you and let's forget all this talk about the Reynolds's," he purred as he took my hand and gently led me out of the kitchen. "We've a lot of planning and packing to do. I intend to make sure you are rested and on your toes. Do you realize how many attendees they're expecting this year?" he cleverly asked diverting my attention.

"Shane Spencer, if I didn't know better, I would think you had ulterior motives suggesting a bubble bath," I teased as he began nibbling my neck.

"I do have ulterior motives," he leered and led the way upstairs. "I love my wife and plan on keeping her very happy."

As we approached the second story landing, the doorbell

rang and all thoughts of a relaxing soak in the tub were suddenly interrupted.

"Were you expecting someone?" he asked as he trotted down the stairs. "Oh, it's Matt and Olivia," he said surprised as he unlocked the front door. "Matt, old buddy, get in here!" he said warmly as he shook the tall detective's hand. They had formed a strong friendship since meeting in Dallas more than two years ago.

"Come in you two," I gestured and invited them into our family room. I was curious as to the reason for this unexpected visit since I'd left Olivia only a few hours ago. Normally she would've been feeding the horses and performing the evening chores around Riverbend Ranch. This wasn't like her to deviate from her strict schedule. Olivia slipped off her boots and left them on the front porch. It was a habit of hers to take off her shoes before entering a house. You never knew what you might track in after working with animals all day.

"What brings you to this part of town tonight?" I asked as I motioned the newlyweds to take a seat on the comfortable sofa next to me. "Is something wrong?"

"You could say that," Olivia said as she sat down.

Shane and I gave each other a quizzical glance as we waited for Olivia to continue. Matt took her hand and squeezed it gently in support.

"I'm so upset, I don't even know if I can even speak right now," Olivia admitted as she turned towards her husband and buried her head into his chest. Matt Lincoln placed his arm around her and looked at us with concern evident on his rugged face.

"Doug Reynolds is under investigation for the misappropriation of campaign funds," he calmly informed us.

"You can't be serious!" Shane said in total shock. "Doug? I don't believe it!"

"Believe it, Shane!" Olivia cried. "And it just keeps getting worse."

"Are you certain of this?" Shane questioned as he quickly sat down in an oversized leather chair. "Where did you hear this?"

"It was reported on the news this evening," Olivia explained. "I had the radio on in the barn while I was feeding the horses and heard there's a full investigation. I can't believe Cassandra has to go through more than she already has. First his infidelity, now he's funneling campaign money. What's next, jail?"

"He's under investigation. That doesn't mean he broke the law. It does mean there were enough red flags to warrant a second look. I'm sure he'll be cleared of any wrongdoing on his part," Lincoln said with authority.

"I wanted to drive over here and let you know as soon as I found out," Olivia told me. "I'm so upset for her right now. If I could lay my hands on Doug Reynolds I would squeeze him until his eyes popped out!" she said vehemently.

"Which is why I drove tonight," Lincoln added. "There's no way I was going to let her drive in this emotional frame of mind. She was ready to head to Nashville and confront Doug," Lincoln chuckled and shook his head.

"What's so funny?" she asked her husband as she lifted her chin defiantly to challenge him. "I can take on Doug Reynolds."

"I'm laughing at the thought of you pulling up in your huge Ford F350 truck at his gated house and demanding he come out and discuss this with you," Lincoln explained.

"So that's why Thomas Simpson at Cassandra's tonight," I said aloud. "This explains why she's been so secretive."

"Thomas Simpson's at Cassandra's? How do you know that?" Olivia inquired as she turned her full attention in my direction.

"I called about the trip to Las Vegas to make sure she's still going," I relayed. "We were on the phone for less than a minute when she said Thomas Simpson had arrived and she abruptly hung up," I said and shrugged my shoulders. "This information may explain why she's been behaving strangely."

"Did the radio broadcast say how the funds were misappropriated?" Shane probed.

"No details, just a blanket statement reporting he was under investigation. Poor Cassandra," Olivia cried. "My heart's breaking for her."

"Have you heard anything about this at the police station?" Shane asked Matt.

"There's been some scuttlebutt around the station, but nothing concrete," Lincoln replied. "I didn't want to say anything prematurely until the facts were known."

"You knew about this?" Olivia said astonished. "And you didn't tell me?"

"I don't report department gossip. The feds were there meeting with the captain, but I wasn't privy to the conversation," he informed his overwrought wife.

"The feds are involved? Oh my stars, this is getting worse by the second," Olivia wept.

"Liv, we don't know anything for certain other than an investigation is underway. That doesn't mean he's guilty. There've been many politicians who were investigated and cleared of wrong doing," I reminded her as I passed a box of tissues in her direction.

"Name one," she challenged as she snatched a tissue and blew her nose loudly. "I can't think of one innocent politician."

"Let me think," I paused and ran a list of names through my head. I was having difficulty thinking of anyone investigated who was found innocent. The collateral damage from this probe would leave Doug unable to continue his bid for governor.

"Precisely, I've made my point," Olivia declared. "He's guilty."

"Liv, it's an investigation. Let it run its course. This is not the Salem Witch Trials," Shane interjected.

"I have no problem trusting but if a man is capable of cheating on his wife right under her nose, he's unethical enough to misappropriate campaign funds," she avowed as she straightened herself upright. "Are you forgetting all the parties and campaign dinners Cassandra and Dixie planned together? They were friends, good friends and this relationship went on for several years. Oh, you can bet if Doug Reynolds could lie to Cassandra for all those years, he could misappropriate campaign funds!" Olivia said aggressively.

"I understand you're upset, but let's not get carried away," I calmly told her. "It's true; when it comes to husbands Doug is a snake in the grass. But one issue has nothing to do with the other. We have to keep an open mind. I'm sure Cassandra is trying to do the same."

"How many more chances is she giving him? How can she know he's being honest about this?" Olivia bemoaned.

"We don't know what she's thinking or planning. And it's probably best we don't," I thought aloud. "She needs our support and friendship more than ever. She'll work through this and make the best decision for herself. I'm sure of it."

"Thank goodness for Thomas Simpson," Olivia declared. "He's a smart attorney and he'll give her good advice," she said sounding a bit more confident.

"Yes, Thomas is tops in my book," Shane agreed. "After what he did for Amelia in Dallas, I'll always be grateful to him."

"He's a straight shooter," I said knowingly. He'd kept me steady when I'd been a suspect in the homicide of my former college roommate, Katherine Gold. Cassandra had flown Reynolds's top attorney to Dallas to help clear my name. She was in capable hands.

"Now that there's an investigation, do you think she'll still go to Las Vegas?" Lincoln wondered.

"She told me tonight she's planning on going. I'll take her word unless I hear otherwise," I reasoned. "I think a trip would be good for her right now."

That was an understatement; first Doug's betrayal with Dixie Beauregard and now a federal investigation. Life had become complicated and ugly for Dogwood's Cove "best dressed diva." Cassandra was a well-respected, brilliant, big-hearted person. No one who knew her would want her to endure this public humiliation. It would be up to "The Traveling Tea Ladies" to make sure her spirits were lifted during this challenging time.

# CHAPTER THREE

"This hotel is stunning!" Sarah sighed as she turned in a complete circle with her head tilted back to take in the view of the Bellagio lobby. More than two thousand hand blown glass blossoms in brilliant hues of violet, tangerine and emerald hung from the eighteen-foot ceiling and formed one of the most well-known chandeliers by artist Dale Chihuly.

"Be careful or you'll get run over by a bellhop," Olivia warned as Sarah kept moving in sweeping circles snapping pictures with her camera. She was completely enthralled with the massive lobby and seemed oblivious to everyone.

"I've never seen anything this beautiful in person," Sarah disclosed as a tear gently escapedthe corner of her eye. "It's so immense and yet so delicate. It looks like Venetian glass."

"Wait until you see the botanical gardens and conservatory. What the gardeners create is amazing," I enthused. "One year I visited and the gardens were overflowing with blue hydrangeas and thousands of tulips. It was spectacular!"

The Bellagio had more than one hundred forty full-time horticulturists to construct the unique and gorgeous displays which featured bridges, ponds and a diversity of flora that continually changed with the seasons. The gardens also hosted daily live musical performances.

"Forget the chandelier and the gardens, I want to see this chocolate fountain I've heard so much about," Olivia interjected. She had her arm draped around Matt's waist as she peered around the lobby looking for the famous chocolate feature. "I've heard it's in the Guinness World Book of Records as the largest chocolate display."

At twenty-seven feet high, the floor-to-ceiling spectacle was enclosed in glass and pumped over a ton of dark, milk and white chocolate to the delight of the Bellagio patrons. Guests could indulge in a sweet or savory crepe, hand crafted chocolates or a custom cake.

"Cassandra's good friends with Chef Jean Philippe who owns the patisserie at the Bellagio," I told Olivia. "I met him at Reynolds's headquarters in Paris when we were working on the tea-infused truffles. He told me his team of one hundred ten chefs creates more than fifteen thousand pastries each day."

"Speaking of Cassandra, where did she go?" Olivia inquired glancing about the check-in area. "We haven't decided who's rooming in which suite yet."

I glanced over to the Concierge station and saw a trim and perfectly coiffed Cassandra chatting with a woman behind the desk. I assumed she was getting information on one of the many shows or five star restaurants Las Vegas offered. She'd seemed her usual outgoing self on the plane and had been attentive to everyone's needs with beverages and snacks. If I didn't know what was going on in her personal life, I'd never guess her husband was in the middle of an FBI investigation. I was pleased she made the trip but was concerned about the façade she presented to everyone.

"I say let's flip a coin," Lucy Lyle suggested. "Imogene and I aren't worried who we bunk with," the spunky gray-haired lady added. She was wearing a conservative black pant suit, taupe blouse and practical ballet flats.

"Don't speak for me," my Aunt Imogene piped up. "I plan on painting the town red, so if you room with me you either need to be ready to party or be a deep sleeper. You know the saying ... 'what happens in Vegas,'" she joked and dug to the bottom of her large leopard tote in search of her fire engine red tube of lipstick. "I plan on making the most of this week if you know what I mean," she winked and applied a fresh coat of lip color.

"I'm here for the World Tea Expo," Lucy reminded her housemate, "not to have some wild fling. I don't mind hitting the slot machines and doing a little card playing, but I won't be up all hours of the night and neither should you."

I glanced over at Shane and shook my head in amusement. I still couldn't figure out how these two ladies had agreed to purchase a home together. Imogene was semi-retired and working part-time in real estate. Lucy had recently sold her tea room to travel more. They reminded me of Blanche Deveroux and Sophia from *The Golden Girls*. Aunt Imogene always dressed in animal prints and stilettos, was an outrageous flirt and had dated almost every eligible bachelor over fifty in Dogwood Cove. Lucy didn't date much, dressed conservatively and rarely stayed out after nine PM. They bickered and argued quite a bit, but despite their differences, they enjoyed each other's company.

"Why come to Vegas if you don't plan on having fun?" Imogene razzed her friend. "Be prepared for some adult fun because I have reserved tickets for us to see 'Thunder From Down Under'!"

"Thunder what? Is that some sort of magic show about the weather?" Matt Lincoln asked.

"Be careful what you ask. You just stepped into the TMI patch," Olivia warned her husband.

"TMI patch?" he asked obviously confused.

"Too much information," she patiently explained. "Watch for it, here it comes," she giggled.

"No Matt, *Thunder From Down Under* is Imogene's idea of fun. It's an all-male strip show from Australia," Lucy said with disapproval in her voice.

"They dress up like firemen and policemen and take it all off," Imogene crowed as she slapped her hands together for emphasis. "I love to pay tribute to our hard-working, hard bodied men in uniform."

"TMI. I've got it now. I'll have to skip that one," Lincoln chuckled and squeezed Olivia's hand in quiet confirmation. "I have a few things up my sleeve for my bride."

"Like what? You're keeping secrets from me and you know I don't like secrets," Olivia moaned.

"Not secrets, surprises," Matt corrected. "If you knew everything, it would take away the fun."

"Back to the rooms," Shane reminded us. "Have we reached a decision as to who is sharing a suite?"

"I don't mind sharing a suite with Imogene and Lucy," Sarah offered. She and Aunt Imogene were very close after their close call with the Andrew Johnson Bridge Murderer. If it weren't for Sarah, my beloved aunt might still be missing. "I'm assuming Cassandra and I will be sharing one-half of the suite since we traveled solo," she explained.

"And that way, the guys can enjoy each other's company," Imogene agreed. "I think we've reached a decision," she concluded.

"I'm so used to sharing a room with Cassandra on our girls' trips, this will seem odd," Olivia confessed.

"We're just down the hall from each other so you two can visit as much as you want," Lucy reminded her.

"I want to keep a close eye on her right now," Olivia told the group. "She's going through a lot."

"If she's sharing a suite with us, you won't have to worry about that. You should see the loungewear Imogene has packed for this trip. I think she's trying to get an invite to the Playboy Mansion to meet Hugh Heffner," Lucy teased.

"You hush, Lucy Lyle!" Imogene laughed and swatted her friend on the forearm.

"What did I miss?" Cassandra asked as she approached our circle. "From the looks of it, the fun has already started," she said as she adjusted her black patent leather Chanel bag over her shoulder.

"Yes the fun has started and will continue in our suite. You're rooming with us," Imogene informed the platinum blonde CEO of Reynolds's Candies.

"Oh, there's been a misunderstanding," Cassandra hesitated. "I've booked a suite in the penthouse. I thought it would be easier to host my business meetings there," she clarified.

"Business meetings? What business meetings?" Olivia probed. "I thought you were here for World Tea Expo and a few days of fun and relaxation?"

"Any time Reynolds participates in a show, we meet new clients and set up dinners and meetings to procure the big accounts. Having the additional space in the penthouse allows me to host private meetings," she patiently said. "I'll make time for fun, don't you worry," she reassured her best friend.

"I guess we thought you'd room with us like always," Olivia said sounding let down.

"Reynolds has a lot riding on this expo if we hope to have our tea-infused truffles carried by some of the larger retailers. I need to stay focused on the business right now, Liv."

I looked over at Olivia and gave her an encouraging smile. I could plainly see the disappointment on her face.

"Let's find our suites, get settled and then explore the strip," Shane said hoping to interrupt the tension. "Since Amelia and I will be busy the next few days, I was hoping we could all get together for dinner."

"Does anyone have a suggestion where to eat tonight?" I asked.

"I vote not to eat at *Thunder From Down Under*," Lincoln jested.

"That's too bad. I think our Dogwood Cove detective could give those boys a run for their money," Imogene said flirtatiously.

"Back off Imogene," Olivia smiled. "He's all mine!"

"What about Olive's?" Cassandra recommended. "Chef

Todd English is a long-time friend of mine and his food is fabulous!"

"Who don't you know?" Olivia snarked. "You and your 'Holly-weird' connections!"

"Those Hollywood connections got our chocolates into the Oscar gift bags the last four years. "You have to rub a lot of elbows to get favors," Cassandra said.

"Speaking of your connections," Sarah interjected, "do you know Jonathan Kirk?"

"Jonathan Kirk, Jonathan Kirk. That name sounds familiar. Who is he?" she asked deep in thought.

"Don't ask. Please don't ask," Olivia pleaded.

"He's the foremost authority on the paranormal. He's written several books on the subject," Sarah explained adjusting her glasses for emphasis.

"Oh, yes. I think I've heard of him," Cassandra recalled.

"He's here for Comic Con and I'm hoping to attend his lecture on the supernatural. He's promoting his latest book," Sarah added.

"Sounds fascinating," Imogene remarked. "There's something about a man who believes in ghosts. It sends chill bumps up my arms just thinking about it," she said pulling her leopard cape closer to her torso.

"You get chill bumps thinking about any man," Lucy joked and looked around the group for affirmation.

"Don't get her started, Imogene!" Olivia barked. "She'll be dragging you to all the haunted spots on the strip. I'm not going this time, Sarah" she warned.

"That's too bad because the Haunted Vegas Tour meets at nine-thirty tonight," Sarah informed her.

"What dear? Haunted Vegas tour as in Las Vegas is haunted? It may be haunted by the ghost of one of my ex-husbands!" Imogene chuckled.

"Please don't tell me you got married in Vegas? That's so tacky!" Lucy pronounced.

"It was a nice wedding. An Elvis impersonator officiated and the witness was dressed like *a Playboy* bunny. That was many moons ago and husband number three," Imogene reminisced.

"Sounds so romantic," Lucy commented rolling her eyes. "And we wonder why it didn't last."

"Back to the haunted tour, Sarah," Imogene cut off Lucy and shot her a dirty look, "tell me more about it."

"The literature claims you might see the ghost of Liberace, Redd Foxx, Bugsy Siegel and visit the 'Hotel of Death' where many celebrities have died of unknown causes," Sarah said barely audible.

"Sign me up. Do I need to change my clothes?" Imogene wondered looking down at her leopard leggings and four-inch high-heeled boots.

"I'd wear comfortable shoes. It's a walking tour," Sarah recommended.

"That means no stilettos," Lucy explained.

"And she'll walk you up and down the entire strip," Olivia warned. "My feet were swollen for three days after our Savannah ghost walk."

"You do exaggerate a tad much," Sarah said defensively crossing her arms. "Don't let her fool you. You should've seen the hair on her arms stand straight up when we visited the Pirate House," she snorted.

"As I recall, we were trying to get away from that drunk leering at us at the bar. I wasn't the least bit scared. There's no way I believe the ghost of Captain Flint walks around the basement of the tavern. They're trying to sell eyepatches and Jolly Roger flags to guileless tourists," Olivia argued placing her hands on her hips ready for a challenge.

"Wow, it's almost time for the Bellagio fountain show," I said glancing at my watch. I was concerned these two might have a free-for-all in the hotel lobby if we didn't immediately change the subject. Sometimes I felt like a kindergarten teacher refereeing a playground game of tag when these two debated. Olivia was very practical, a die-hard skeptic and brutally honest with her opinions. Sarah was naïve, easily led and one of the kindest people I knew. The two were close friends but their differences often times led to misunderstandings and hurt feelings.

"The bellhop says we have a beautiful view of the fountain from our suite," Shane announced as he took my hint. "He's already headed to the rooms with our luggage, so we'd better get moving if we want to see the show."

Our entourage took the elevator up to the twelfth floor. As the large doors opened and we departed, Cassandra held the open door button and remained inside the elevator.

"Aren't you coming?" Olivia asked expectantly. "The show starts in a few minutes."

"I'll be right there. I'm going to meet the bellhop at my suite and I'll be back down. I'll make it in time. Why don't you open up a bottle of bubbly and we can toast our trip?" she suggested and waved goodbye as the doors closed before Olivia could object.

"She's acting very weird," Olivia said candidly.

"Honey, she probably needs to check on things first. She'll be right back," Matt reassured her as he placed his arm around her tiny waist.

The two were such a cute couple. Matt Lincoln towered well over six feet and she barely reached his chest. She was the yin to his yang. Before he had met Miss Olivia Rivers he had all but forgotten life existed outside the Dallas police precinct. He'd worked diligently to rise to the rank of detective and his heavy caseload left very little down time. Olivia had opened his eyes to a different pace of life. Being outside and working with the horses and children who took lessons at Riverbend Ranch had helped him not only get in touch with his Texas roots but also gave him a new perspective on life. His transition to the Dogwood Cove Police Department had been an adjustment, but Matt Lincoln had never seemed happier.

"This is our suite," Shane announced as he took out the key card.

"We're right next door," Sarah called out as she found the door number.

"Hurry up, put your things down and join us for some champagne," I said to the three single ladies. "You don't want to miss the fountain show. It's breathtaking!"

The suite was furnished in calming tones of ivory and beige with dramatic chocolate brown walls. A long ottoman that could comfortably seat three was placed in front of the towering window overlooking the lake and fountain area.

"I can see why they named this the Grand Lakeview

suite," Olivia commented as she approached the panoramic view and looked down. "This is unbelievable!"

"Whoa, check out this steam room," Lincoln yelled from one of the two master suites. "And there's a television above the bathtub. Now this is luxury!"

"Great, now I'll never get him out of the bathroom," Olivia chuckled. "Don't get too comfortable in there, Matt. We've got a show and some champagne for a toast," she reminded him. "I guess he's claimed our side of the room," she smiled and gave me a hug. "I'm excited we'll be sharing this huge suite with you. It'll be good for the guys to spend some time together."

"Shane has been eager for this trip ever since Matt agreed to come. I don't play golf, so now he has a buddy for tee time and tea time," I joked. "I know you were looking forward to bunking with Cassandra but I'm sure she'll be hanging around here a good part of the time," I said hopefully fingering one of her long auburn spiral curls.

There was a knock on the door and I rushed to open it. "How's your suite?" I asked as the trio piled into the living area.

"Magnificent," Imogene spoke up. "It looks similar to yours except we have two queen beds in each of the master bedrooms. It's going to work out for the three of us to share the suite. Lucy and I will share one side and Sarah has the other. I feel so fancy with all the marble and granite in this hotel!"

"She's already had her boa out and pranced in front of the bathroom mirror," Lucy said with a deadpan expression on her face. "Thank goodness she's too old to enter a

*Toddlers and Tiaras* pageant."

"That's why it's called 'Toddlers', not 'Spinsters and Tiaras,'" Imogene stated.

I started to giggle and covered my mouth with my hand. I could picture Aunt Imogene in the talent portion of the show twirling a baton and giving her trademark pose of one leg extended daringly copying the fashion of Miss Angelina Jolie. If there were a *Toddlers and Tiaras* pageant for seniors, she'd have a huge fan base.

"You two are so wicked," Sarah smiled and embraced them both. She loved these two ladies as much as I did and it seemed the roommate situation was settled. Everyone was pleased with their arrangements.

"Cassandra will miss the show," Olivia said with concern visible on her face. "Should we call her?"

"She'll be here. Let's open the champagne and make a toast," Shane pushed forward. He knew how upset we all were about Cassandra's decision to have a separate suite. The less said about the subject, the better. Rooming together had made our trips special. The laughter, the stories, the camaraderie we shared on our many travels had woven a tapestry of great memories over the years.

"To 'The Traveling Tea Ladies,'" I held up my champagne flute as Shane continued to pass each of us a glass, "and to our 'Traveling Tea Men!'"

"Here, here! To the men!" Imogene raised her glass to her lips and took a long swig.

"I'm not sure I want to be referred to as a 'Traveling Tea Man,'" Matt clowned. "That sounds like some sort of British *Food Network* program."

"Good one, Matt," Shane agreed and slapped him on the back.

"It's starting!" Sarah squealed as she looked out to the water below. "Oh my goodness, it sounds like their playing *Lucy in the Sky with Diamonds*," she pointed out as we watched the water shoot up more than fifteen feet in the air. It was a ballet set to music, but instead of ballerinas, the dancers were thousands of waters shooters and lights moving in time. It was an awesome sight.

"There's a show every thirty minutes," Lucy said knowingly. "They'll play some classical music like Rachmaninoff and then switch it up with Frank Sinatra. I never get tired of watching this," she shared as she gazed at the dancing water below.

"I wish Cassandra was here," I whispered in Shane's ear. Olivia was right. It wouldn't be the same without her sharing our suite. I hoped whatever was keeping her was not more bad news. She desperately needed a fun and relaxing trip. I would do my best to help her remember how to do both.

# CHAPTER FOUR

"**D**inner at Olive's was wonderful," I mentioned looking into the mirror. It had been such a pleasant evening shared with friends. Cassandra had called and decided to meet us there instead of joining us in our suite. Olivia had pouted for a short time, but once the appetizers of fig and prosciutto flat bread, tuna tartare and beef carpaccio were presented, all hurt feelings were forgotten.

"Last night was perfect," Shane purred in my ear as he helped me to hook my heart-shaped diamond pendant around my neck. It had been an anniversary gift from him and I touched it as I admired the necklace in the mirror.

"I'm nervous about the tea championship," I divulged. He turned me to face him and looked deeply into my eyes.

"This is a time for us to celebrate," he reminded me. "All the hard work is behind us. We sent in our tea sample months ago. We're here to celebrate our first World Tea Expo as a new vendor and the rest is out of our hands. Let's meet as many people as we can and introduce them to our beautiful teas. I'm counting on your marketing background to get us some new accounts."

"I plan to sweep the flavored iced tea category this year," I said as I planted a kiss on his lips.

"We better enjoy a big breakfast because it's going to be a long day," he said. We would be setting up our booth in the exhibition space and preparing for the thousands of attendees expected tomorrow. I had a long checklist, comfortable shoes, a huge stack of invoices waiting to be filled out, and thousands of business cards to hand out in my Smoky Mountain Coffee, Herb & Tea Company tote bag. We were ready or so I hoped.

I grabbed a lightweight sweater in case the show room was cold and opened the door only to be greeted by Aunt Imogene and Lucy waiting outside.

"Get a move on Amelia! You've got a booth to set up," Imogene fussed at me.

"Where's Sarah?" I inquired as I stuck my head out the door and glanced towards their suite.

"She's downstairs with Olivia and Lincoln," Lucy replied. "You know how hungry that little slip of a cowgirl gets. She was anxious to get downstairs for breakfast and beat the rush. She came by to get Sarah about a half hour ago." She ran her fingers through her gray hair and adjusted her quilted tote bag across her chest.

"Sarah's up early this morning," Shane commented. "I would have thought last night's ghost tour would have worn her out."

"She was energized after that tour," Imogene spoke up. "I've never seen anyone so serious about ghost sightings. She had a little notebook, some kind of electrical gizmo..."

"It's called an EMF meter," I recalled from our tour of Tennessee's oldest and most haunted town, Jonesborough.

"Yes, an EMF meter and some thermometer gadget for detecting a change in the air temperature. That's supposed to indicate the presence of a spirit," she continued.

"It means the night air is getting cooler," ever practical Lucy said.

"So, did you see any ghosts?" Shane asked as we walked towards the elevator. He was dressed in khaki slacks, comfortable shoes and our company's dark green shirts with our Smoky Mountain logo.

"Not a one," Lucy quickly answered. "I saw a lot of riff raff on the streets and I learned a lot about the escort services around here."

"What? What in the world are you talking about?" I gasped as the doors closed and began our ascent to the penthouse floor.

"Yeah, it's very different at night. These people hand out these little cards with women's pictures and profiles on them. It's vile, just downright disgusting!"

"You do have to be careful," Imogene agreed. "I think I'll stick to the hotel casinos and the shows. Don't tell Sarah, but I didn't feel comfortable walking around at night on that tour. I wouldn't want to hurt her feelings because she had such a good time."

"It wouldn't be a bad idea to stick to the hotels and let Lincoln and I take you around at night," Shane agreed. "This isn't Dogwood Cove," he warned.

We walked to the end of the hallway and knocked on Cassandra's door. She didn't open it right away and we stood patiently looking at each other.

"Do we have the right room?" I asked Shane as he knocked a second time a bit louder.

"Yes, this is her suite. Maybe she didn't hear me the first time."

"Maybe she's with Olivia and Sarah at breakfast already," Imogene submitted as she adjusted the enormous shoulder pads of her zebra print overcoat.

"I'll call her cell phone," I volunteered as I dug into my tote bag. I had her number programmed and called her.

"That's strange, she's not answering," I told them. "Do you think maybe she's already at the exhibition area setting up the booth for Reynolds's Candies?" I thought aloud. She'd be handing out samples of the raspberry tea-infused truffles and blood orange tea-truffles we'd collaborated on.

"It's possible, but I expected her to answer her cell phone. Let me knock one more time in case she overslept," Shane told me and rapped on the door more loudly.

"We'll catch up with her later," I said as a sinking feeling grew in the pit of my stomach. Cassandra was the consummate business woman. She was always on time, in fact often early, always dressed for success and the best deal closer I had ever witnessed. Something was amiss and I knew it.

"I'm calling Olivia," I said as I pushed talk. "Maybe she knows where she is."

Olivia answered on the first ring. "Good morning, tea champion!" she sang into the phone. "Hurry up and get here before there's nothing left on the breakfast buffet."

"Is Cassandra with you?" I asked.

"No. Last night she said we could swing by her room

and get her on our way. Are you going by?" she asked as she chewed her food and talked into the phone.

"We're here and there's no Cassandra answering."

"Knock again or better yet, call her," Olivia recommended.

"We've done both," I answered. "Where could she be?"

"Maybe she went to the fitness room for an early morning workout," Lucy surmised.

"She said last night the Presidential Suite has its own fitness room," Imogene recalled.

"I'm sure she's at the exhibition center setting up and has her phone on vibrate. We'll catch up with her later," Shane concluded.

"We can't find her, but we'll catch up with her later I'm sure," I repeated to Olivia over the phone.

Just then the door opened. Much to my shock and surprise, a sleepy looking silver-haired man appeared in the doorway wearing a navy blue silk robe.

"Good Morning, Shane!" he said looking a bit startled. "I thought I heard someone in the hallway."

"Who is it?" Olivia demanded in the phone.

"It's Doug. Doug Reynolds," I told her as I hung up.

# CHAPTER FIVE

"*I* really didn't know what to say," I shared with Olivia, Sarah and Matt as we joined them at breakfast. "I haven't seen him since the news of his affair broke. I hope he couldn't tell how uncomfortable I was to see him." I added honey to my English breakfast tea and stirred my spoon nervously in circles inside my teacup.

"I want *him* to know how uncomfortable we are around him," Olivia seethed. "After what he's done, why should we act like everything's fine?"

"Did anyone know Doug was coming this weekend?" Lincoln questioned as he glanced around the table at our group.

"No, I didn't. But then again, why should we assume he wouldn't come?" Sarah speculated. She looked adorable today wearing a 1950's inspired dress reminiscent of June Cleaver. The robin egg blue color of her outfit contrasted beautifully with her brown eyes. Her waist was cinched with a wide matching sash. A pair of black ballet flats with bows on top completed her ensemble.

"I assumed he was out of the picture," Olivia spoke up as she took another bite of her pancakes. "Doug never comes to these events. He didn't fly in with us yesterday, so why is he here?"

"Maybe he's here to help this weekend," Shane analyzed. "He could be trying to put his best foot forward and mend fences."

"Mend fences? Are you serious Shane?" Olivia sputtered as she wiped her mouth. "He's a two-timing no-good son of a…"

"Liv, you can't fight her battles for her," Matt admonished his wife. "She has to make her own decisions when it comes to her marriage. What goes on behind closed doors is none of our business."

"I don't want to make Cassandra uncomfortable," I pointed out. "If those two are working it out, I want to make it easy on her. They've invested a lot of years into their marriage. Maybe this whole thing with Dixie is water under the bridge."

"I don't know honey," Aunt Imogene interrupted. "Once a man cheats you can forgive, but no matter how hard you try, you never forget," she advised. "Marty and I weren't able to stay together after I caught him with that waitress down at the Tick Tock. I thought I was going to go postal on the two of them."

"That would've been interesting," Lincoln chuckled as he took a sip of his orange juice. "Why any man would run around on you is a mystery to me," he smiled and reached across the table to pat Imogene's bejeweled hand.

"He's a keeper Liv," she beamed at his compliment.

"I know. I'm fortunate," she agreed. "Where is Cassandra?"

"Doug said she was already on the exhibition floor. We'd better head over there, Amelia," Shane advised as I took one last sip of tea.

"What are you doing today?" I asked the group.

"Lincoln has planned a special outing just for the two of us. I'm not sure what he has up his sleeve but I've been told to drink a lot of water. Mysterious!" she smiled and leaned over to kiss her husband.

"You must be getting a couple's massage. You have to drink a lot of water to flush the toxins after a massage," Imogene reasoned as she posted a Tweet on her rhinestone encrusted phone.

"Don't you ever put that thing down?" Lucy said disapprovingly. "It's rude to have that out at the table."

"And you must be 'Miss Manners.' I'm Tweeting what we are doing today," Imogene bantered back.

"What are you doing Aunt Imogene?"

"Shopping of course and playing the slot machines. Caesar's Palace has some beautiful shops I know Lucy would love to browse."

"And you Sarah?" I turned and asked my dear friend. "Are you going shopping too?"

"I planned on going to Comic Con and getting Jonathan Kirk to autograph my book," Sarah revealed. "I'm so excited!"

"Is today the lecture?" I asked confused.

"No. That's in a few days. Today is a meet and greet with some of the science fiction writers. I'm hoping to strike up a conversation with him and if I'm lucky, get his picture," she said beaming. "He's considered the notable authority in his genre."

"Notable nut case," Olivia muttered under her breath as she dabbed her mouth with a napkin.

"What?" Sarah asked leaning closer to Olivia.

"Let's get going," Shane said grabbing my hand looking for a quick exit. "Whoever is available for dinner, send me a text and we'll meet up."

"You got us out of there just in time," I joked as we went to the lobby of the hotel. We'd walk the few short blocks to the expo located at the lower end of the strip in the Las Vegas Convention Center. Cassandra had made arrangements for our cargo to be delivered to the expo loading dock. We needed to claim our boxes and begin the monumental task of unpacking and setting up the booth.

"I had no idea there would be so many exhibitors," I said in awe as I looked around the massive room. There were row upon row of booths representing all the major tea brands including Harney & Sons, Rishi Teas, and the Republic of Teas. Tea wholesalers representing the major tea producing countries of Kenya, China, India, Japan and Taiwan were also setting up their stalls. The fragrant smell of tea filled the air and delighted my senses. I felt right at home.

Every tea implement imaginable was represented from sugar cubes, to tea cozies to gorgeous porcelain Spode and Wedgewood tea pots. It was a tea lover's fantasy land.

"I hope we'll have time to look around later," I said to Shane as we found our row number and headed toward our space. "There's so much to see and many classes I'd like to attend."

World Tea Expo offered a variety of classes taught by experts in the tea industry from business boot camp to the proper method of tea cupping. Marketing authorities, branding specialists, health and wellness professionals, and tea authors would all be conducting educational seminars for expo attendees.

"I'm hoping there's very little time for anything except filling orders," Shane beamed his trademark smile and hurried down the aisle. We'll be lucky to grab a quick bite of lunch," he prophesized.

"There's Cassandra," I waved at my rail-thin friend. She was busy stocking the temperature controlled display cases with an assortment of chocolates. She had on a Reynolds's Candies apron over a chocolate brown mohair sheath dress. Her dark caramel boots and dark brown tights were the perfect touch.

"Did you sleep in?" she teased as we approached our adjacent area. "I've been here for hours already. I had a couple of guys bring your boxes over with our equipment."

"Thanks Cassandra," I said giving her a quick hug. "You didn't have to do that!" I did appreciate the time it would save us making several trips with our dolly to get everything over to our designated spot.

"You look great as usual," Shane said giving her a quick kiss on the cheek. "Even when you're working, you still dress for the boardroom."

"You never know what business contacts you may run into," Cassandra agreed. "How's everyone this morning? I decided to skip breakfast and get an early start."

"That's what Doug told us when we stopped by your

room," I casually mentioned to her. "I didn't know he was making the trip."

"Hmm, yes, yes, he decided at the last minute to come," Cassandra replied as she continued to place candies inside the display. She avoided looking at me and kept organizing the silver platters filled with truffles.

"More guys to play golf," Shane chuckled and turned towards our boxes.

"I'm sure he'd enjoy that Shane," Cassandra said as her face relaxed a bit. I could tell she seemed to be stressed about the situation. I couldn't help but think she was worried how her friends would react to Doug after his secret affair with Dixie became common knowledge. As much as I didn't want to be around him, I would make the effort for my friend.

"This weekend is very important to Reynolds. I am hoping the tea-infused truffles are a hit with spas, hotels, gift shops and tea rooms. That would be a boost for business," she chatted away. "And with this economy, every new account matters."

"I'm nervous about our small company competing with the giants of the tea industry," I admitted as I looked across the aisle at the other vendors. "If we could place in either the hot or iced tea categories, it would make all the difference in gaining the respect of our peers and new business accounts"

"You worry too much," Cassandra laughed. "Your teas are wonderful and top quality. It doesn't matter the size of your business, it's the final product that makes the difference. Don't forget that," she said knowingly. "We make the extra effort to use the finest ingredients available to craft our chocolates and you can taste the difference. Those judges will be able to do the same with your teas."

"You're always so positive. Thank you," I grinned and began organizing the table display.

"Don't forget the new product category," she reminded me. "Reynolds and Smoky Mountain may sweep the competition this year with these orange blossom oolong truffles," she said taking a bite of one. "I never tire of these," she said closing her eyes and savoring the delicate blend of dark chocolate with the subtle flavoring of tea.

"I am partial to the raspberry truffles myself," Shane remarked. "Don't rule those out either."

"You can't go wrong with either one," I agreed and began assembling the large banners with our Smoky Mountain Coffee, Herb & Tea Company logo imprinted on them. "This is going to look fabulous," I said with excitement in my voice. "Zack did an outstanding job on these new signs."

"Let me finish opening those since they're so tall," he suggested. "You can get the baskets filled and work on the tabletop details."

"Are you insinuating I can't manage the banners?" I jested.

"Absolutely not," Shane quickly responded. "I think I'm better at some tasks and you're much better at others. Together we make a great team."

"You're a fast thinker, Shane Spencer," Cassandra joined in on the playful discourse. "Never tell a woman she can't do something."

"I know better. I've been trained," he teased me and continued working efficiently. Before long, the signs were erected, the baskets and displays were filled with row after row of our assorted loose teas and coffees and we were ready. We stepped back to survey our work.

"I like our plan of having the teas by categories," Shane said, "lightest to darkest, white to blacks."

"It makes sense to do it in that order," I concurred, "and having the coffees displayed by country of origin was a smart idea. I think our patrons will easily find what they're wanting. Offering a different sample each half-hour will keep them coming back by the booth to try another variety."

"How's it coming along?" I asked Cassandra who was single-handedly putting the Reynolds booth together. "Do you need help?"

"I appreciate the offer, but I'm just about finished," she told me.

"Are you ready to take a lunch break? I've been dying to eat at Serendipity's and try their famous frozen hot chocolate! You'd love it," I encouraged her.

"I've actually already made plans for lunch. Another time?" she answered.

"Sure. Are you coming back after lunch?" I inquired.

"I'm not sure. It will depend on how my lunch meeting goes," she said nonchalantly.

"Hello, Cassandra!" a dapper looking gentleman called out. He approached her and kissed both cheeks in greeting.

"Rick, how are you? You look well," she beamed as he took both her hands in his.

"And you look smashing as always," he returned the compliment.

"Amelia, you remember Rick Green from the Savannah Fancy Foods Show?" she reminded me.

"Oh, yes! How are you?" I recalled Rick was the CEO of Aztec Chocolates, one of Cassandra's competitors. The two were long-time friends and traveled in the same circles.

"This is my husband, Shane Spencer," I said in way of introductions. "Rick is the CEO of Aztec Chocolates, the company that is opening the chocolate drinking bars in all the major cities across the US," I reminded him.

"Nice to meet you," he said enthusiastically shaking Rick's hand. "I don't suppose we could talk you into putting one into the mall in our small town of Dogwood Cove?"

"I'm not stepping on Cassandra Reynolds's toes," Rick said shaking his head. "She'd have my hide if I did that!"

"You're right, I would!" Cassandra honestly said. "Rick is taking me out to lunch," she told us. "Are you ready?" she asked as she linked her arm in his.

"It was nice to see you, Amelia and nice to meet you, Shane. Shall we my lady?" he waved goodbye as he whisked her from the booth.

"Those two look cozy," Shane observed.

"Yes, yes they do. You don't think this is more than just a business lunch, do you? I'm not one who normally speculates, but I sensed there was some electricity in the air."

"I think you're hoping there's some electricity after what Doug did to her," he stated. "Let's set our personal feelings aside. I'm sure this has to do with chocolate and business."

"You think what you want," I spoke up. "Doug Reynolds has taken her for granted. I'm sure Rick Green is not the first man who's thought about pursuing her. I wouldn't blame her for wanting to have a little male attention."

"What do you know about this Rick Green?" Shane said cautiously.

"Not much. His public relations director used to work for Cassandra and the two have known each other for years. They're business rivals but seem to be on friendly terms."

"Very friendly, I'd say," Shane commented as we looked down the aisle and saw Cassandra walking with her head resting comfortably on Rick's shoulder. He had his arm around her in an caring way.

What in the world was going on? Was Cassandra dating someone already? If she was dating Rick, what was Doug doing in Las Vegas?

# CHAPTER SIX

"*I*'m not going to say anything to the girls," I said decidedly as I applied fresh makeup for our evening of dinner at Picasso's and the show "O" by Cirque de Soleil. I had heard the water gymnastics, artistry and live music were second to none.

"How do we know she isn't meeting with Rick Green to discuss going to work for Aztec Chocolates?" Shane threw out the possibility as he adjusted the knot in his burgundy tie. I had to admit, he looked dashing tonight in his navy blue suit.

"You don't think she would leave Reynolds, do you?" I said as my mouth fell open in shock. "I guess I never considered she might leave." I sat down on the ottoman in the large bathroom and felt suddenly deflated. "She would leave Dogwood Cove if she went to work somewhere else."

"He'd be a fool not to try and talk her into jumping ship. After all, it's a ship with some damage. I'm sure word of Doug's infidelity has generated gossip within the industry and she's vulnerable right now. It makes perfect sense he'd be trying to lure her away with all her knowledge and experience to run Aztec Chocolates alongside him."

"I don't agree with you on this. I don't think Cassandra will leave Reynolds. She's helped to build it up. Why would she leave it to be run by Doug when he's involved in politics? He doesn't have the time," I argued.

Shane pointed out, "He's being investigated by the FBI. He may have to step down from politics. If Doug and Cassandra divorce, why would she want to stay on at *his family's* business?"

"But Doug's here this weekend. That doesn't seem like a marriage on the road to divorce. And let me say for the record, I think the company would be better off with Cassandra in charge no matter what the circumstances. She's the one who spearheaded the Oscar gift bags, the recent write-ups in *Gourmet Magazine* and the four-page spread in *Southern Living*. And that's just the tip of the iceburg."

Only Cassandra and Doug knew what the next step for them would be. I knew decisions involving a large corporation were carefully weighed and she might be offered a severance package to step aside should there be a divorce. But that was my point, up until now there had been no mention of a divorce. I wasn't sure if they had officially separated. What I did know was that Doug was in Nashville most of the time and now he had shown up for the weekend. It was clear as mud.

"Let's focus on enjoying the evening and let the Reynolds work out their issues. Here we're discussing the state of their marriage and the state of their business when it's not our place to do so. I love Cassandra like a sister. I want what's best for her. Doug I don't feel so warm and fuzzy about at the moment," I admitted and stood up to inspect my outfit before we joined Olivia and Matt in the living room. "Do you like my dress?"

"Do you have to ask?" Shane said with a seductive grin on his face. He rubbed my bare arms and spun me around to take a complete look at the strapless tulle sheath that hugged my hips perfectly. The soft rose color complemented my fair skin.

"I better keep a close eye on you tonight," he warned as he kissed my hand and led me to Olivia and Matt standing by the large panoramic window.

"It's about time you were ready. I'm starving!" Olivia complained.

"You look gorgeous," I remarked as I beamed with pride. Olivia had gone from ranch hand to desert goddess with her pumpkin colored backless halter dress and copper jewelry. She had never looked more radiant.

"What? This old thing?" she joked and placed her hand on her hip. "Just something I picked up for the trip."

"Speaking of trip, how was today?" Shane inquired of Lincoln.

"So you knew about it, then?" Olivia accused the boys.

"I thought girls were the ones who couldn't keep secrets," I joined Olivia in ribbing them. "What trip did you go on?"

"I planned a guided trail ride in the desert," Lincoln said proudly. "I knew it would be something she'd never forget."

"And there was a feast waiting for us when we reached our destination," Olivia continued. "There were buffalo burgers, steak fries, grilled corn with black beans, and the best sour cream pound cake with fresh fruit that I have ever eaten. It was wonderful!"

"That sounds heavenly," I sighed and patted Matt on the arm. "Good job. You won her heart on both the food *and* the horse fronts."

"The views were breath taking. I'll have to share my pictures with you after dinner," she proposed.

"Speaking of dinner, let's round up the three ladies next door and head out," Lincoln directed. "I think everyone is looking forward to the show tonight. From everything I've read, the diving stunts are incredible."

We left our room and knocked next door. Imogene greeted us wearing a leopard print sequin top underneath a black satin jacket and matching pants. Her signature animal print bag was over her shoulder. It was large enough to carry her wardrobe for the week. I enjoyed watching what she would pull out from the enormous tote. It always reminded me of the scene from *Mary Poppins* where Mary pulled the lamp out of her satchel.

Lucy was casually dressed in a comfortable pair of black pants and a black cardigan sweater. She had opted to wear a slightly brighter shade of pink lipstick for the evening.

"Ladies, you look lovely," Shane said and showered them with attention. "Is Sarah coming?" he asked confused.

"She called and said she would meet us there and to add one," Imogene informed us.

"Add one as in add one more guest?" Olivia asked surprised.

"Yes, she's bringing a guest since Cassandra can't make it tonight. Something about a business meeting, so Sarah will use the ticket to the show for her guest," Imogene explained.

I looked over at Shane with a knowing expression. Her business meeting must have gone longer and better than planned. Maybe he was right about Rick Green. Maybe she was planning on leaving Reynolds or maybe they were more than friends. I was disappointed that she hadn't called herself to say she wouldn't be joining us. We'd all been looking forward to tonight's show.

"And the mystery guest is…" Shane trailed off.

"She didn't say, but she did say she had the best day of her life at Comic Con and she couldn't wait to tell us all about it," Lucy continued. "I'm crazy about that girl. They don't get any sweeter than Sarah."

"I'd rather hear about Comic Con then sit across from Doug Reynolds and make small talk," Olivia said truthfully. "I'm sorry Cassandra isn't coming tonight, but I didn't count on Doug tagging along for the week."

"Try to let it go, Liv," Matt encouraged his wife. "She's going through a very difficult time. Maybe they're having a nice dinner together and trying to move on."

We exited the massive elevators and made our way to the lavishly appointed Picasso Restaurant located within the Bellagio. The interior was decorated with arched doorways and elaborately lit walls designed to showcase original works by the artist Pablo Picasso.

"I've never seen a Picasso in person," Imogene said admiring the abstract paintings as we were escorted to our table. We'd be dining outdoors with a view of the fountains of Bellagio tonight.

"This is lovely," I whispered to Shane and squeezed his

hand. "It's perfect. I don't think I will ever tire of watching the water dance."

"I thought you might enjoy sitting outside. The weather is perfect. This will be an evening to remember," he predicted as he kissed the top of my head.

"Sarah, doll, there you are!" Imogene sang out loudly as Sarah pushed back her chair to give my aunt a warm embrace. "And who might this handsome fellow be?" she piercingly announced to all the other diners on the patio as she plopped her gigantic animal print bag on the table next to Sarah's guest.

"Imogene, let me introduce you to someone very special," Sarah smiled broadly. "This is Professor Jonathan Kirk, author of *A Ghost's Guide to Understanding the Modern World*," she proudly announced.

"Professor Kirk," Imogene said as he stood and took her hand warmly between both of his.

He was smartly dressed in a tan three-piece suit and bowtie. An antique pocket watch was tucked inside his vest. His salt and pepper hair was neatly pulled back in a ponytail.

"Enchanted," he said as he looked over Imogene from head-to-toe. "Sarah you never told me you had such a beautiful sister," he prattled.

"Aren't you charming," Imogene stated as she basked in the compliment.

"And these are my good friends from Dogwood Cove," Sarah continued with the introductions. "Shane and Amelia Spencer, Lucy Lyle, Matt and Olivia Lincoln."

"It's a pleasure," he said as he politely shook hands with everyone gathered. "Thank you for including me this evening. It's not every day I have the pleasure of such beautiful company," he said smoothly.

"Good grief, all the flowery compliments," Olivia confided quietly as she took a seat next to mine. Matt pushed in her chair and sat down next to his bride.

"Professor Kirk, how did you two meet?" Lucy Lyle inquired. I was glad she had broken the ice so we could find out more about Sarah's latest friendship.

"Please, call me Jonathan," he insisted as he turned towards Lucy. "We met this afternoon during a press junket at Comic Con. I was there for pictures with the fans when I looked across the room and saw this beautiful creature," he divulged putting his arm across the back of Sarah's chair. "She literally took my breath away."

"Oh, Jonathan, stop. You're embarrassing me," Sarah said as her cheeks blushed. She bashfully looked around the table with her head slightly lowered, gauging our reaction to her admirer's compliments.

"I'm not surprised in the least. Sarah is a very special lady and near and dear to my heart," Lucy grinned and looked towards Sarah nodding her head in approval.

"Hmm," Olivia interrupted by clearing her throat. "I'm curious, Professor, where do you teach?" She took a dinner roll out of the bread basket and began tearing bite-size pieces and devouring them. She stared intently at Jonathan's face waiting for an answer.

"I am the Dean of Paranormal Psychology at the New Mexico School of Paranormal Studies," he said confidently.

"They have a school for paranormal studies?" she asked incredulously. "I've never heard of it."

"That doesn't surprise me in the least," he calmly responded. "We're a small university with a few hundred students. We like to stay 'under the radar,' so to speak," he jested. "I'm hoping this book tour will provide exposure for our program and educate the public about the dimensional co-existence of the supernatural."

"Would anyone care to begin with a cocktail this evening?" a petite blonde server graciously asked our table.

"I'm going to need one," I disclosed to Shane. "This could be a long night. I'd like a chocolate martini," I told the server.

"That sounds wonderful. I'll have one too," Imogene agreed.

"Sarah, Lucy? Would you care for a cocktail? We're in Vegas after all," Shane suggested.

"I'll have one of those 'in and out lemontinis,'" Lucy spoke up.

"None for me," Sarah declined. "I want to be clear headed tonight so I can remember every moment," she beamed.

"Dear me," Olivia muttered. "She's in over her head already," she said dropped her napkin purposefully. "I'm worried about her, Amelia."

"Gentlemen?" the server asked.

"I'll have a Devil's Handshake," Jonathan spoke up.

"That sounds delicious! What's in it?" Sarah questioned.

"It's sweet and sour with tequila, ginger puree, and a splash of pineapple juice. You should have one," he urged.

"Devils handshake about sums up how I feel," Olivia said quietly with her napkin in front of her mouth. "I have goose bumps right now," she divulged.

"Behave," I warned her and tried my best to ignore her remarks.

"I think I'll wait until my entrée to order some wine," Shane told the server. "Thank you."

"I'll wait as well," Matt agreed.

"My stomach is suddenly queasy," Olivia told us. "I think I'll pass this evening."

"What's wrong? Too much sun today?" Lincoln asked anxiously.

"Something like that. I'll be fine," she reassured him. "I'm curious about this ghost school. Tell me more about it," Olivia continued interviewing Jonathan Kirk.

"Paranormal studies," he corrected. "There is a distinct difference," he said benevolently. "Paranormal by definition means things outside of scientific explanation or scientific methodology and can encompass a broad range of topics including teleportation, alien life forms, crop circles and poltergeists. A ghost is a manifestation of a soul or spirit. The two have very different meanings," he systematically explained as he placed his fingertips together to form a triangle.

"Thought provoking," Imogene said enthralled with our newest addition.

"I'm confused," Lucy Lyle spoke up. "What is it you do at this school? You teach parapsychology? What is that exactly?"

"It's the study of extra-sensory perception. It's like that sixth sense you have or intuition about an event or situation before it happens. Many of us have this ability."

"I'm having an intuition right now," Olivia said sarcastically. "Sorry, Professor Kirk, but I'm not drinking the crazy juice."

"Liv, please," Sarah implored. "For once, be open to what Jonathan has to share."

"It's alright," he calmed Sarah. "I'm used to having a skeptic or two in the crowd."

"I've gone on several of these so called 'ghost tours' with Sarah and not once have I seen anything confirming the presence of anything supernatural. It's folklore or urban legend as far as I'm concerned," Olivia pronounced crossing her arms and leaning back in her chair.

"I've met many individuals like you who've come to my workshops and after a couple of field trips have become believers. It's hard for many to put faith in something unseen until they personally have experienced a paranormal phenomenon first hand," he explained.

"Here are the cocktails! Thank you," I told our server, hoping we could focus on something other than the current discussion which in my opinion was not boding well.

"What a beautiful presentation," Imogene said as she admired the chocolate rim on her martini glass. She took a sip and proclaimed, "It's like having dessert first!"

"This is wonderful," I agreed as I indulged in the Godiva chocolate liqueur. "Oh the fountain show is beginning."

I was relieved to have a few minutes of distraction from the present conversation. Olivia seemed hostile towards Professor Kirk. Perhaps she was because Sarah, Imogene and Lucy had all seemed to fall under his spell of flowery compliments and highbrow dissertation on the supernatural. I too was a skeptic, but I was polite enough not to embarrass Sarah by making a guest uncomfortable. She'd have to figure these things out for herself. My hope was she wouldn't get hurt in the process.

Someone as prominent in the world of the supernatural as Professor Jonathan Kirk would likely have a great deal of influence over Sarah. I had to remind myself these two just met and it didn't necessarily mean anything more than dinner and a book signing. I knew her track record with men and how easily she gave her heart and trust. I didn't want to see her go through that again and be taken advantage of in any way.

"We'd better order if we want to make it to the show on time," Shane suggested as the fountains were once again still.

We had decided to indulge in the "pre-theatre" menu Picasso's offered its guests. We could choose between warm langoustine salad or poached oysters as a starter. Sautéed filet of halibut with asparagus and hollandaise sauce or milk fed veal chop with rosemary potatoes and au jus were the entrée selections followed by a signature dessert. It was a fantastic menu and as I finished my dark chocolate gelato with toasted marshmallow and graham cracker, I found myself relieved the rest of the dinner conversation had steered clear of ghosts and the paranormal.

The show starts promptly at nine thirty," Shane reminded us as we finished our last few bites of yumminess. "I'm very pleased we were able to get golden circle seating. We'll have to thank Cassandra for pulling her strings."

Cassandra. I'd forgotten about Cassandra and Doug during dinner with our new guest. She'd be missing the show. We'd catch up tomorrow during the expo. Hopefully she'd share with me how her lunch with Rick Green had gone.

"She's fine," Shane reassured me as if reading my mind. Maybe Professor Jonathan Kirk was right. Maybe there was more to this sixth sense or intuition than I realized. I was starting to get the feeling something was terribly wrong.

# CHAPTER SEVEN

"*I* ordered room service. They should be here shortly," Shane yelled over the blasting hair dryer. We awakened at six thirty AM to eat a good breakfast and get ready for the exhibition.

"I'm excited about the start of the expo this morning and the announcement of the tea championships. I hope I can manage to eat," I admitted nervously. I quickly brushed my hair back into a sleek pony tail and finished with a light mist of hair spray.

"No matter how it turns out, we learned a lot by entering the competition. We'll be ready for next year. You never know, we may sweep the whole show!" That was my Shane— ever optimistic and thinking ahead. I'm sure he'd already organized his thoughts as to which teas we should enter in each category next year.

"I'll be done with my makeup in just a minute," I smiled as I expertly applied a coat of mascara.

"I think I heard the doorbell," he said exiting.

I was left alone with my thoughts as I replayed the

events of last night over in my mind. Sarah seemed almost hypnotized by the attentions of Professor Kirk. I still hadn't formed an opinion of him. The whole idea of devoting one's life to the study of the paranormal was beyond my comprehension, but I did admire the fact he was following his passion. He was obviously an educated man and an accomplished author, but I didn't feel as though I had a good read on him. I'd decided to proceed with caution. Maybe after I attended his lecture I'd have a better understanding and sense of him.

"Madame, your breakfast waits," Shane announced as I cleared my head.

"Great!" I followed him into the living room and was surprised to see Matt and Olivia up and dressed for the day. "Good morning," I greeted them. "I didn't expect you'd be joining us this early."

"My clock is still set on Eastern time," Olivia explained as she helped herself to some breakfast potatoes. "I'd be finishing the morning feeding about now."

"I forget you get up so early. What have you two planned for today?" I asked as I sat down to the dining table. "A little gambling, maybe shopping?"

"Lincoln wants to rent a car and drive to the Hoover Dam," Olivia answered as she slathered butter on her toast. "This was a good idea to order breakfast in the room. It gives us a chance to talk privately about *'The Nutty Professor.'*"

"Is that what you've nicknamed him?" Shane asked amused as he poured himself a cup of coffee. "Come on, Liv. Give the guy a chance. He seemed harmless."

"He reminded me of a traveling medicine show salesman

with his malarkey about the supernatural, two-dimensional theologies, and sixth sense voodoo talk. People like him give credible institutions a bad rap."

"I've been thinking about last night too," I acknowledged. "I can't put my finger on it, but I also have concerns about Professor Kirk."

"Not you too?" Shane said sounding deflated. "This guy doesn't stand a chance passing the board of approval."

"Do we even know if he's truly a professor? Maybe it's an honorary degree," Olivia responded defensively. "Is the New Mexico School of Supernatural Studies an accredited university? These are questions to ask."

"Which one of you is Daphne and which is Velma?" Matt spoke up.

"What?" I asked confused.

"You know, *Scooby Doo?*" he joked. "You don't need to worry about Sarah. She's a big girl and this isn't a serious relationship. So she met this very eccentric author and she's a big fan. Sharing dinner and a show with her probably made her whole trip. Let her enjoy herself without making a federal case against him. The guy is harmless," he lectured as he helped himself to scrambled eggs and sausage.

"I agree with Lincoln. He seemed like a nice guy," Shane added.

"I hate the buddy system," Olivia seethed. "You dudes always agree with each other, especially if you feel another man is being misjudged by the female sect," Olivia argued. She stabbed a sausage with her fork and began cutting it.

"Olivia's right. I've never heard of the New Mexico School of Supernatural Studies. Don't you find that to be odd?" I asked.

"And I find it odd that they didn't come back after intermission last night. That was an amazing water show. I couldn't tear my eyes away from the stage. I still can't figure out how they rigged it so one performer walks on water and the next minute another performer is diving from twenty feet above into a deep pool. It's amazing how quickly they changed the water level."

"It was an excellent show. On that, I will agree," Shane said waving his napkin like a white flag of surrender.

"So you don't find it strange they left in the middle of the show?" Olivia continued.

"Maybe he got an important call," Matt submitted.

"Yeah, maybe there was a ghost that needed his immediate attention," Olivia retorted. "And Sarah needed to leave with him without saying anything to us?"

"That's uncharacteristic of her. I would've expected her to say something," I concurred.

"The way your aunt and Lucy were fawning all over him, maybe they wanted some time alone," Shane theorized.

"I believe the professor was doing the fawning," Olivia recalled. "He used that old line about 'is this your sister' to flatter Imogene and Lucy. He's like a snake charmer and I'm afraid Sarah may be charmed hook, line and sinker!"

"And if she is, what's the worst thing that could happen?" Matt reasoned.

"She could shave her head, join his cult of parapsychology weirdos, move to New Mexico to live on his commune and we'd never see her again. This guy is going to break her heart and I know it!" Olivia babbled.

"It was dinner and a show. You worry too much," Shane told her.

"I hope that's all it ends up being," I spoke up. "Sarah is so naïve. She's been vulnerable ever since her breakup with Jake White. She's obviously star struck by Jonathan Kirk."

"You're treating Sarah likes she's a child and not your peer. She can handle herself quite well. I saw that firsthand when she rescued your Aunt Imogene. Sarah's a smart lady," Lincoln reassured us.

"Not always smart about matters of the heart. And I think it's safe to say we are concerned about all of our friends when it comes to that," I said thinking of Cassandra.

"We women have to mull things around," Olivia explained impatiently. "You guys can go out and have a beer with someone and you're best bros. Women don't operate like that."

"Is that what you think about us? We can be bought off with a beer?" he asked in mocked astonishment.

"Quit that. You know what I'm talking about. Like this whole thing with Cassandra and Doug. Right now if he asked you to go play golf with him, you'd probably pretend nothing was wrong and pick up where you left off before the whole Dixie fiasco," Olivia theorized.

"I'll admit. Guys don't like to poke in each other's private lives," Shane agreed. "But things will never be the same between Doug and me. I'll be cordial, polite in public, but as far as giving him the impression that he could treat Cassandra like that and still have a close friendship with me, not happening!"

"So you do take sides," Olivia pressed. "That surprises

me. That goes against the guy code."

"I take my marriage vows seriously. Under no circumstance was it right for Doug to cheat. And knowing Cassandra as well as I do, I have nothing but the highest regard for her. They made a great couple and though I will miss Doug socially, I don't consider him to be much of a friend. I've reached out to him several times the past few months and he's never bothered to return my calls," Shane confided to us.

An abrupt knock at the suite door interrupted our conversation.

"Who could that be this early in the morning?" I thought aloud as I jumped up to answer the door.

"Probably your aunt and Lucy just turning in after a long night at the blackjack tables," Shane jested.

"Good morning!" Sarah enthusiastically greeted us as she entered the suite. She looked adorable wearing red peddle pusher pants and a black knit top with cherries embroidered along the scoop neckline.

"Have you eaten?" I inquired as I indicated the table with the remnants of sausage and eggs.

"I'm so excited, I couldn't eat a thing," she politely refused and sat down to join us. "Do you have coffee?"

"Of course we have coffee. I thought you were more of a tea drinker," Shane said surprised. "Here, try our Jamaican Blue Mountain Estate. I think you'll enjoy the well-balanced acidity and smooth chocolate finish," Shane said with his polished salesman confidence.

"Practicing for today are you?" Olivia teased.

"You're right Shane. Normally I drink tea. But I got to

bed late last night and I need something to perk me up if I'm going to the expo," Sarah answered as she added cream and sugar to her coffee.

"A late night, huh? You and the professor seemed very cozy at dinner," Olivia observed.

"Jonathan was showing me the manuscript for his next book. I lost track of the time," Sarah said as a slight blush rose up her face.

"Showing you his manuscript? Is that the code word these days?" Olivia kidded as she continued eating her breakfast.

"It wasn't like that," Sarah said protectively. "I find Jonathan to be fascinating and we have so many things in common. In fact, that's why I'm here. I wanted to invite you to join us for a skydiving trip this afternoon."

"Skydiving? Are you out of your mind?" Olivia shrieked banging her cup down loudly.

"Jonathan is licensed with the United States Parachute Association. He has thousands of jumps under his belt and he guarantees the views of the Hoover Dam, the Colorado River and the Vegas strip are unbelievable!" Sarah prattled.

"It wouldn't matter to me if he were Special Forces and had parachuted in combat, there's no way I would go skydiving!" Olivia objected.

"I've been skydiving before. It's a rush," Matt interceded. "You should think about tandem jumping for your first time."

"Et tu Brute? Have you totally lost your senses? I can just picture myself free falling and ending up looking like a flattened 'Mr. Bill.' No way, no how!"

" 'Mr. Bill?'" Lincoln tilted his head confused.

"You know from Saturday Night Live? You remember the clay man that was always smashed by a steamroller or a car? Never mind!"

"Shane, Amelia, how about you?" Sarah asked hopefully. She took a sip of her coffee and looked expectantly at us for our response.

"I wouldn't mind tandem skydiving," Shane answered. "I'm sure the views are spectacular from that vantage point. How high is the jump?"

"Fifteen thousand feet," Sarah answered.

"Shane? Are you crazy?" I asked in total shock. "There's no way I'm jumping from an airplane. What if my parachute didn't open?"

"That's why you have a certified instructor tandem jump with you and there's always a safety chute for emergencies. It's very safe," Sarah said knowingly.

"And suddenly you're an expert on parachuting?" Olivia said snidely. "If you two guys want to be idiots and skydive, at least make sure your life insurance policies cover accidental death from jumping fifteen thousand feet above the ground," Olivia suggested.

"We talked about seeing the Hoover Dam. This is a great way to do it," Matt spoke up. Think about it Liv."

"All I can think about is the expo and I don't want to be late. Sarah, I'll get back to you with our answer," Shane said pushing his chair away from the table.

"I've already invited Lucy and Imogene," she said.

"Aunt Imogene is seriously considering this?" I asked astonished. I knew she was young at heart, but jumping from a plane at her age? I wasn't sure if that was a good idea.

"Lucy said she would be part of the land crew and Imogene is a definite yes. She said it was on her 'bucket list.'" Sarah explained.

"I have a 'bucket list' too, but free falling from that height is not one of them," I admitted. "I think I'll stay with Lucy on the nice, safe ground and be waiting with a bottle of champagne," I offered.

"Shane and Amelia are a yes, or at least half a yes. Lucy and Imogene are going. How about it, Liv? I think it would be a once in a lifetime experience," Sarah pressed.

"Matt? What do you want to do? If you want to jump, I'll go, but I'm not leaving the ground."

"I think it sounds like a plan!" Lincoln decided. "We can do some sightseeing today and meet up for skydiving after the expo. What time?

"If we meet here by four PM, that will give us plenty of time to go through the training class and jump before sunset. It'll be a gorgeous time of day and hopefully the temperatures will cool down a bit by then. Be sure to wear athletic shoes and they will provide the safety goggles, jump suit and harness."

"How about an adult diaper?" Olivia said with all seriousness.

"The expo finishes at five PM. I'm sure I can manage the last hour by myself and then drive out to the airport," I suggested.

"I can help this afternoon," Olivia spoke up. "I'll help close your booth and ride with you."

"Sarah, we should invite Cassandra and Doug," I said thoughtfully. "I don't want to leave anyone out."

"That's a good idea. I'd like to see Doug wet his pants jumping from that high," Olivia joked. "It would make my day."

"Text me or call me and let me know so I can confirm our reservations," Sarah said, pleased she'd persuaded her friends to join her.

We briskly walked the three blocks to the Las Vegas Convention Center. I could feel the tension in my neck and shoulders increasing as I thought about the forthcoming announcement of the North American Tea Championships at noon. I was determined to enjoy every moment of this weekend no matter what the outcome of the competition.

As we entered the exhibit hall my senses were immediately stimulated by the vegetal aroma of tea and spices. There were over two hundred tea companies, beverage specialty products, gourmet food vendors and every conceivable tea implement represented. People were scurrying around making last minute adjustments to their booths in preparation for the thousands of eager attendees. This year the expo had partnered with the Healthy Beverage Show to offer two tradeshows. The three-day event promised to provide good exposure for Smoky Mountain Coffee, Herb & Tea Company.

"Good morning, Cassandra!" I called out as I rushed into our booth and pulled an apron over my head. I cinched the tie and went over to greet my friend.

"It's going to be an excellent show. I can feel it in my bones," Cassandra spoke enthusiastically. "I'm sorry I missed the show last night. I hope everyone enjoyed themselves."

"We did but we missed you. Did everything go well

with your meeting?" I wondered. She seemed to be feeling chipper, dressed in all black from head to toe. Her quilted jacket was adorned with a diamond bumble bee broach. She looked chic and confident today.

"My meeting ran a bit later than I expected, but went great. Are you ready for the announcement at noon?" she asked quickly changing the subject. I looked over at Shane with a suspicious glance that was immediately understood. Cassandra was going to be tight-lipped about her lunch with Rick Green.

"Yes, I'm ready," Shane said assuredly. "Before I forget and the morning gets away from me, I have a special invitation for you."

"An invitation? I'm all ears," she beamed.

"Would you and Doug join us for tandem skydiving later today?" Shane asked as he placed the assorted willow baskets filled with our signature coffees and teas out on the tables. "It would be fun, Cassandra. Think about it!"

"Skydiving? You're serious?" she asked as she tilted her head back and gave a throaty chuckle. "Unless they have designer jumpsuits, I don't see any reason why I would go."

"You can wait at the airport with me if you're not comfortable jumping," I suggested. "I thought I'd bring champagne to celebrate. Please consider coming. It'll be fun," I encouraged my slim friend.

"What about Doug? Do you think he might be interested?" Shane queried. I had to give him points for being nice enough to include Doug.

"Doug won't be available," Cassandra said forcefully. "He's returned to Nashville." She furrowed her brow and I could see the tension spread across her face.

"He's already left? That was a short trip," I spoke without thinking.

"Yes it was, but you know Doug! He's always jetting off here or there. He's been called back for an important vote," she said with forced politeness. "And so here I am ready to face the throngs of tea lovers who want to sample our delicious chocolates."

"The booth looks great," Shane said cheerfully. "Think about the skydiving and join us. Even if you don't want to go up in the plane, it would be fun. And you haven't met Sarah's latest friend, the professor."

"Sarah has a new friend? I did miss a lot at dinner last night. A professor you said?"

"She's mentioned him, Jonathan Kirk, the author of the book on the paranormal?" I reminded her.

"Oh, yes, I remember her saying something about that. I didn't realize she knew him. I thought she was trying to get him to autograph a book or something like that."

"She met him at Comic Con and brought him to dinner last night," Shane filled her in. "You should have seen Olivia's face when he started explaining the difference between ghosts and the study of paranormal psychology."

"That conversation was priceless, I'm certain!" she laughed. Her bright mood had returned and I made a mental note not to bring Doug up again. Whatever was going on between the two of them, he had disappointed her by cutting his trip short.

"We're going to the airport after the expo this afternoon," I informed her. "Aunt Imogene, Matt, Sarah, the professor, and Shane are tandem jumping. Lucy, Olivia and I are providing the cheerleaders and champagne. It'll be one of the days you won't soon forget. Please say you'll come!" I hugged her and waited for her answer.

"Why not? I could use a little fun right now," she disclosed. "Here comes the crowd. Hello, would you like to try a sample of our tea-infused truffles?" she offered an interested attendee. "They're made with orange blossom oolong tea and dark chocolate."

# CHAPTER EIGHT

"Are you sure about this Aunt Imogene?" I asked as I watched her step into her jumpsuit.

"Stop worrying about me, Amelia. I sat through the safety video. It's going to be a piece of cake," she reassured me. "Plus Professor Kirk gave me a few pointers on the drive over. He's such a nice man."

"Where's the rest of the group?"

"They're inside packing their parachutes. Shane told us the good news, sweetheart, congratulations!" she said and hugged me hard.

"Third place is respectable for a first-time entry," I said proudly. "We can get a lot of press and attention from the award. Next year we'll place even higher," I predicted. I was proud our blackberry bramble tea had been received so well. We had entered it in both the hot and flavored iced tea categories.

"Are you sure you don't want to jump, dear? Tandem jumping seems like a no-brainer. The instructor does all the work. You just hang on for the ride," she told me as she applied a spritz of her Red Door perfume.

"I've never heard of anyone applying perfume before a skydiving jump," I commented.

"You haven't seen my partner. He's a very handsome gentleman. A lady always wants to put her best foot forward," she reminded me as she closed the locker holding her tote bag and belongings.

"I'll try to remember that," I smiled as I walked out of the ladies locker room and searched inside for Shane. He was busy talking with the instructors and Professor Kirk.

"There you are Amelia. I was hoping you would get here before we took off. Did we have much business after I left?"

"We did have several tea rooms that stopped for samples and signed up for our mailing list. We stayed busy up until the very end."

"Great! This is Paul, my partner today," he said as he introduced us. "Paul this is my wife, Amelia."

"So nice to meet you," I greeted and firmly shook his hand. "And I see everyone is partnered up and ready to go," I noted glancing around the small waiting area. Matt was standing talking with a large dark haired man suited up for the jump and the gray-haired instructor I assumed was Aunt Imogene's partner.

"We're all partnered up except for Jonathan. He's jumping solo." Shane told me. "He's logged so many jumps he could practically do it in his sleep."

"Jonathan's been skydiving with us for years," Paul spoke up. "He's one of the best."

"That's what Sarah's told us. I was hoping to hear you

were one of the best, Paul, since my husband's life is in your hands."

"You have nothing to worry about," Paul reassured me. "I've completed thousands of jumps and not one of my students has been hurt other than a sprained ankle from a rough landing."

"Yes, the safety video said it was more dangerous to drive in your car than to skydive. You have nothing to worry about, sweetheart," Shane reassured me.

"I believe it with all the texting and driving these days," I agreed. "I've got the champagne icing so we can celebrate a successful jump!"

"We're fueling the plane now and getting the gear together," Paul reported. "The best place to watch the dive is from the observation tower. It has the best view," he indicated pointing to a flight of stairs. "We even have a monitor set up where you can view the footage live from our helmet cameras. You're welcome to wait upstairs or outside. I'll leave it up to you."

I looked around the waiting area and spotted Cassandra deep in conversation with Professor Kirk. It appeared the two were becoming acquainted.

"And this is an automatic activation device or AAD. It calculates the rate of speed you're falling and the exact moment the parachute should open. Every diver needs one because in case of an emergency, it will automatically open your chute."

"A very important piece of equipment indeed," Cassandra said agreeably. "And how long have you been interested in skydiving?"

"I've been an avid skydiver for twenty-plus years. Now I've added this place to my list of favorites," Jonathan proudly said. "New Mexico has beautiful places to jump and I manage to go almost every weekend since I belong to a skydiving club. I'm so glad Sarah invited all of you to come. It's always 'the more the merrier' when it comes to skydiving!" he smiled widely and placed his hands on his hips.

"Speaking of Sarah, where is she?" I asked looking around the room. Lucy and Imogene were talking with Imogene's instructor. Matt was going over some last minute preparations with Paul and Shane with a very nervous Olivia looking over his shoulder. I didn't see Sarah anywhere.

"She's probably in the ladies locker room," Cassandra guessed. "Now tell me more about this book tour you're doing."

"Thank you for asking," Jonathan Kirk beamed under the attention. "My latest novel is called *Bridging the Transition* and I have my fingers crossed that a movie option will be picked up."

"Seriously? How wonderful!" Cassandra cooed. "Are you writing the screenplay?"

"It may be a bit premature to share this news, but yes, I have a deal to write the screenplay," he boasted. "That's one of the reasons I've been promoting the book so heavily. If the book sales are strong, the movie version is a sure thing."

"And that's good publicity for your school as well," Cassandra pointed out.

"And good publicity for your next novel," Sarah interjected emerging from the dressing room. "It's a sequel to the last book, so this may turn into a multiple movie deal," she shared.

"There you are! I was looking for you. Did you enjoy the expo today?"

"I did. I drank tea up to my eyeballs. I learned a tremendous amount in my classes, especially the tea cupping workshop. It was fascinating," she shared as she touched Professor Kirk's arm affectionately. He put his arm around her waist and grinned. These two were definitely cozy.

"Did you attend the tea blending class? That was my favorite," I recollected. The combinations of herbs, seasonings, edible flowers, essential oils, fruits and nuts could literally translate into thousands of different flavorings of tea. I never tired of experimenting and trying new amalgamations.

"I'll be going to the tea blending seminar tomorrow morning after the seminar on social media and the tea industry. I'm going to have to ask your aunt for some pointers," Sarah joked as we turned and observed Aunt Imogene texting her friends and updating them on Facebook and Twitter about her skydiving adventure. This would be the talk of Dogwood Cove for certain!

"Did you hear Jonathan may have his book turned into a movie and possibly a second movie deal is in the works?" Cassandra blabbed.

"And you should know I've asked Sarah to come out to New Mexico to do research with me on my next book," he said and kissed her cheek. "With her skills as a research librarian and her keen interest in the paranormal, she's a perfect fit."

My eyes widened in shock as I realized how fast this relationship was moving. Sarah would leave for New Mexico? What about the tea room? Would this be a short-term project or require a move on her part? I didn't feel comfortable with how quickly this man had turned her life upside down. But she seemed so happy. I didn't want to rain on her parade.

"Let's load up," Paul shouted and I rushed across the room to give Shane a kiss for good luck. "Don't break a leg," I joked and brushed his hair from his eyes. "I'll be watching from the monitor."

"Get the champagne ready. We're toasting our third place award and a successful jump," he called over his shoulder. I watched amused as the jumpsuit clad ensemble left the waiting room.

"Ladies, to the tower!" I led the way up the stairs followed by Olivia, Cassandra and Lucy. Olivia's red ostrich boots made a loud clanging noise on the metal and cement steps. They complemented her red and turquoise Santa Fe Skirt perfectly.

The observation area was set up for the best view of the giant bull's eye that marked the landing target for the skydivers.

"Paul, Shane's tandem partner, has a camera on his helmet to record the jump," I shared with them. "I can't imagine how nervous they must be right now."

"Imogene's Facebook and Twitter pages are going crazy!" Lucy commented looking at Imogene's rhinestone encrusted phone. "She asked me to update everyone during the jump. I hope she doesn't end up fracturing a hip or something worse. What was she thinking?"

"She was thinking of trying something new and exciting," Cassandra spoke up. "And why not? She's not getting any younger. She doesn't want to look back on her life and have regrets," she trailed off. She leaned over the rail and looked wistfully off into the distance.

"I don't regret skipping the jump," Olivia remarked. "I've tried several dangerous sports like bull riding, but something about plummeting from the sky at a high rate of speed seems like a nightmare! How can you get a thrill from that? I guess it's because you're cheating death."

"I feel like I cheat death every time I eat out these days. It's preposterous what they put in our food! I'm sticking with ordering my organic beef from Riverbend Ranch," Lucy endorsed.

"I appreciate that," Olivia said sincerely. "We have pre-sold all of our beef before the next slaughter. I've been amazed at the number of people on the wait list. If I had more acreage, I'd have a larger herd."

"I'm sure Dan is managing the farm quite well while you're gone," I said making small talk. "I know it's hard for you to be away for more than a day at a time."

"This is our first trip since we got back from the honey-moon. It was time to take another vacation. I know when I return we'll be busy with our summer horseback riding camps, so I'm not feeling guilty about taking some time for myself right now," Olivia responded. She was a micro-manager and usually uneasy about leaving her horses and herd for more than a day. I was glad to see a more relaxed side of her on this trip.

"Yes, make time for each other," Cassandra advised. "Before you know it you'll look back and wonder where the time flew."

"Are you feeling alright, Cassandra? You seem down-hearted," I observed.

"I'm fine, I'm fine. Just a little sentimental today," she said shaking off her mood and placing a practiced smile on her face.

I paused and thought about the date. I scanned my memory banks and then it dawned on me. Today was her anniversary with Doug! How could I have forgotten? And he had flown back to Nashville.

"It's your anniversary today, isn't it?" I quietly asked approaching her slowly. "Is that why Doug came out to Las Vegas? You two were celebrating your anniversary?"

"You could say something like that," she said cryptically. "At least he thought it would be a good idea."

"You didn't think it was a good idea?" Olivia asked hesitantly.

"I can't hold this in any longer. My attorney has told me not to talk with anyone, including my dearest friends. But I need to get everything off my chest before I explode. No, I didn't know he was coming. He sprang it on me at the last minute. That's why I got the separate suite. I had a text message from Doug saying he was on his way. He thought it would be a nice way to celebrate our anniversary," she confided in us.

"But he left. What happened?" I cautiously nudged her for details.

"I feel like such a fool," she cried and placed her hands

over her eyes. "He tried to convince me that he'd made a terrible mistake and wanted to give our marriage a second chance." She began sniffling loudly and dabbing her eyes with a tissue. I had not seen the confident boardroom woman so broken up before.

"For some reason, you don't believe him," Lucy spoke up.

"No, I don't. Not when I found out the real reason he was here," she continued. "His campaign manager suggested he patch things up with me to look good for his constituents when the investigation becomes public."

"So he wants you to stand by his side when the media starts buzzing around him," Olivia speculated. "You don't feel as though he regrets his involvement with Dixie?"

"I think he regrets it," she hiccupped through sobs. "I think he regrets getting caught. And now he has the audacity to expect me to hold his hand while he is scrutinized in the tabloids. What a spineless thing to ask!" she said angrily.

"I'm glad you're finally talking about this," I said rubbing her back and doing my best to comfort her. "We've all been worried about you but didn't want to meddle."

"Thank you for saying that. I needed some time to think straight. There's the company to consider and my position at Reynolds. I don't want to make a snap decision that will have a domino effect on what I've worked so hard to build."

"What are you going to do?" I calmly asked. "Is there a chance you two can salvage your marriage?"

"I don't know how I feel right now. I do know that Doug hasn't explained his relationship with Dixie to me. He immersed himself in his work in Nashville when I found out. It's almost as though he were running away from facing me.

And I've put everything on hold: my emotions, my worries, my fears. It's like my feelings are on autopilot waiting for Doug to make up his mind."

"Why wait for Doug to make up his mind? Did he consult you first when he decided to step outside the marriage? I'm sorry to be so blunt, but this is about you and what you want," Olivia sounded off.

"It's not that easy, Liv. We have a history together. And honestly, I haven't seen Doug for the past few months. He's confined himself to his condo in Nashville, and I've carried on with the company and taking care of our home. I think we've been avoiding each other."

"Sounds like it," Lucy interjected, "but Olivia is right. Doug should be doing his best to make amends, not avoiding you. I would be insulted if I felt like his trip to Vegas was nothing more than a political front."

"Believe me, I'm furious with Doug right now," Cassandra admitted. "I sent him packing when I realized the true motive for his visit. When he started telling me what to wear for the press conference next week, I knew he was covering his bases. We had a terrible argument."

"He wanted to go over your wardrobe with you?" Olivia screeched. "Who does that?"

"Someone concerned with his public image. Here I thought he had remembered our anniversary and was making a romantic gesture. He spent most of his time strategizing on the phone with his team. He assumed everything was back to normal because he said he was sorry. Do you realize how long I've been waiting for him to explain to me what happened?"

"Sorry is just the first step," Lucy said knowingly. "You two needed some time to talk and be open with each other about what has transpired and the feelings on both sides. I'm sure you have many unanswered questions."

"Yeah, like when did you start having an affair with my event planner and how long did this go on?" Olivia angrily recalled.

"He has yet to answer any of my questions. He thinks he can just waltz back into my life and pick up where we left off."

"What are you going to do?" I wondered. "Are you going to publically support him during the investigation?"

"I haven't decided yet what to do. I've a lot to consider right now. If the FBI charges him and he's found guilty, Doug will be looking at jail time. I don't want to see that happen to him."

"What exactly is the FBI accusing him of?" Olivia queried.

"My attorney has advised me to say as little as possible, but I can tell you he's being charged with misappropriation of campaign funds," she disclosed.

"Oh dear," Lucy said with concern evident on her face. "You're being hit from all sides right now, aren't you?"

"I feel battered and bruised," she agreed. "This has been an ordeal for me. I can't recall anything so painful."

"So that's why you've had the meetings with Thomas Simpson," I said relieved. "I was thinking you might be stepping down at Reynolds."

"I've considered it," Cassandra said matter-of-factly. "I've been offered a few positions."

"Doug really screwed the pooch this time," Olivia

commented. "He's going to end up losing the best thing that ever happened to him and to his family's business."

"So your lunch with Rick Green was a business proposition?" I sighed putting the pieces together. She nodded her head in affirmation. "Shane and I thought it would be a smart move on the part of Aztec Chocolates to snag you."

"Was it that obvious? I thought you'd assume Rick was trying to wine and dine me," Cassandra guessed.

"We thought that was a possibility too, especially when you didn't join us for dinner at Olive's and the show."

"Was he trying to wine and dine you?" Olivia supposed arching her eyebrows seductively. "Rick's no fool. You're a very attractive woman and he's single."

"I'm not going there. I'm a married woman," she laughed nervously.

"Unhappily married woman," Olivia reminded her. "Is it possible Rick wants your relationship to be more than business?"

"Stop. You're getting carried away," she scolded Olivia. "Rick Green and I go way back. We've been business colleagues for years. We have a mutual respect for each other and nothing more."

"If you say so," Olivia said crossing her arms and shaking her head playfully. "I'm just saying, Rick Green has eyes in his head. You're a beautiful woman and he notices that, I'm sure."

"Look, there they are!" I screamed as the monitor was filled with a live feed. Huddled around the open airplane door were Sarah, Imogene, Matt and Shane strapped to their jumping partners. The wind was blowing them back as they hung on to leashes looped from the ceiling of the plane in preparation for the jump.

"Can we hear anything?" Lucy asked inching closer to the monitor.

"I don't think so," I guessed. "I bet its cold."

"Look at Sarah," Olivia chuckled. "She's so excited she's jumping up and down. She looks like a little kid."

"And there's the professor next to her. He seems pleased he convinced her to go skydiving." Lucy remarked.

"I believe he could convince her to do just about anything," Olivia mumbled almost inaudibly.

"What was that dear?" Lucy asked her.

"Nothing, nothing at all," Olivia answered.

"I know something when I hear it and I heard it in your tone. You don't care for him," she surmised.

"I didn't say that. I just think things are moving too fast and you know Sarah falls hard. I'm protective of her," Olivia explained.

"He seems nice enough. Did you hear about his possible movie deal?" Cassandra took up for him.

"Movie deal? And you believed him?" Olivia snorted.

"That's what he told me. Amelia heard him too," Cassandra countered.

"That man was blowing smoke rings up your bloomers," Olivia deduced. "He's a snake oil salesman and nothing more. He was probably going to ask you to help him with your 'Holly-weird' connections."

"Stop calling my friends by that name," Cassandra said wearily. "There's no way he could've known I have connections in Hollywood."

"Don't count on it. Sarah has loose lips," Olivia said shrewdly. "I'm sure he knew more about you than you realize. Have you ever heard of the Internet? You can't keep much a secret anymore."

"There goes Matt and his partner," I said getting their attention. "Wow that looks exciting!" I watched as Matt and his companion flattened out spread eagle and began their free fall.

"I can't look!" Olivia screamed covering her eyes. "Tell me when it's over and he's safely on the ground."

"Get your hands down and watch. He's fine. He's having a ball!" Cassandra fussed at her best friend.

"Imogene's up next," Lucy cackled and clapped her hands. "This is hilarious! She's talking to the camera and we've no idea what's she saying."

"Look, she's doing the thumbs up sign," I smiled as I watched my brave and youthful aunt as she jumped wildly out of the plane. "She did great!"

"Sarah's next," Olivia called out. "There she goes. It looked like she hesitated for a brief second. I know I would."

Professor Kirk stepped forward to take his place in the doorway. He gave the camera a quick thumbs up and dove out the door. Shane and instructor Paul were last and were filming the divers below them as everyone grabbed onto each other's arms to form a circle in the air.

"How fun!" Cassandra squealed. "I should have gone up with them."

"There's always tomorrow," I sighed as I continued to watch the monitor closely. One by one the chutes began to open and the skydivers were abruptly jerked up by their harnesses as their parachutes formed a billowing mushroom shape above them.

"How beautiful," Cassandra exhaled as we watched their progress. "Wait, I'm only counting four chutes open."

I moved up closer to the monitor and checked. "You're right, Cassandra. Someone is late opening their parachute."

"The professor told me everyone has an AAD that automatically opens the chute in case someone forgets to pull the ripcord," Cassandra informed us. "I'm sure it'll open momentarily."

As we continued to watch, we began to see one diver continue to fall straight down while everyone watched helpless.

"It's not opening!" I screamed as I continued to watch in horror. "Open, come on open!"

"What's going on?" Olivia yelled. "Who is it? Is it Matt?"

"No, Matt is right here," I showed her pointing to the screen. "There's Imogene and Sarah and Shane's partner is filming. It has to be Professor Kirk!"

"Heavens to Betsy! I thought he was an experienced diver," Lucy shuddered. "I can't watch this! Please tell me his chute opened," she said turning away from the monitor.

"Come on, come on!" I shrieked as I watched riveted. "Open, open, come on open!"

The airport emergency crew began scrambling towards the target area. They too had been viewing the live footage and decided to take action in case the parachute remained closed.

"All we can do is pray," I spoke softly as a tear began to roll down my cheek. My heart sank as I knew the impact from such a high fall would kill the professor instantaneously. Poor Sarah was witnessing her new friend plummeting to his death. And before I had time to blink, the crew was out on the field next to the lifeless body of Jonathan Kirk.

# CHAPTER NINE

"How is she?" I asked as I entered the suite.

"She's finally sleeping," Imogene answered in low tones. She appeared drained and her eyes were puffed-up from crying.

I was grateful Cassandra had moved down from the penthouse into the suite to lend Sarah much needed emotional support. We were all shell-shocked from witnessing the professor's accident. Being together seemed to make the nightmare more bearable.

"I thought you'd be at the expo," Lucy spoke up.

"I'm taking a break. Shane's managing for a while without me. Honestly, my heart's not in it today. I couldn't sleep last night because I keep seeing the fall over and over in my head. I still can't believe this happened," I said as I moved over to the sofa and sat down. I ran my hands through my hair and took in a deep breath attempting to calm my nerves.

"It's all over the papers and television this morning," Imogene said quietly. "I've kept the TV off so she doesn't see it blasted everywhere."

"That's good thinking. We've got to keep her preoccupied right now. Even though she didn't know him well, they'd developed feelings for each other."

"Poor Sarah," Lucy empathized. "Watching him plunge to his death is something I won't soon forget. She's taking it hard."

"And so did the instructors. They'd known Jonathan for years. They must be feeling horrible about what happened," I imagined. I know I did and I felt ashamed for some of the remarks I had made about the professor. No one deserved to die like that.

"The only solace I have is knowing he didn't suffer," Imogene remarked as she crossed her legs and gazed out the window. "It's unimaginable to think what flashed through his mind in his final moments. I hope he's at peace," she cried softly.

"We've got to stay strong for Sarah," I encouraged them. "They've announced a memorial for the professor will be held at Comic Con tomorrow. I know it would mean a great deal to her if we attended."

"Count me in," Lucy spoke up. "This is breaking my heart," she said and turned away to compose herself. Lucy wasn't one to show her emotions.

"I'll be there too," Imogene added. "Cassandra's being here has been such a help. It's made all the difference in the world having her back."

A sharp knock on the door brought our conversation to an abrupt halt.

"Who could that be? I hope they didn't wake her up with that loud knocking," Lucy complained. "Yes?" she said cracking open the door and peering out.

"Detective Keith Kane," a tall man stated flashing his badge to Lucy. "I have a few questions regarding the death of Jonathan Kirk." She unchained the door and ushered him into the suite.

"Detective, I'm Lucy Lyle and this is Imogene Smith and her niece Amelia Spencer. Please come in and have a seat."

"Thank you. First I want to extend my condolences," he said solemnly and cleared his throat. "I understand you were witnesses to the event."

"Yes we were," I said shaking my head. "It was horrific!"

"What a tragic accident," Imogene added. "I can still see him falling when I close my eyes," she trembled involuntarily.

"You were one of the skydivers?" he asked checking his notes. "And Ms. Lyle and Mrs. Spencer you were both watching from the observation area correct?"

"Yes," I answered for all of us.

"Did you notice anything out of the ordinary?" the detective asked Imogene first.

"What do you mean?" Imogene seemed muddled.

"Was the professor agitated or upset in anyway?" he questioned.

"No, quite the contrary. He was excited. He was introducing us to our first skydive and he seemed ecstatic about the jump. Nothing appeared to be out of the ordinary," Imogene expounded.

"Who was present at the skydiving center?" he continued probing.

"Our group and the skydiving instructors. Why do you ask?" I bristled as I feared we were in for bad news.

"Its standard fact checking," Kane reassured me. I've listed the diving party consisting of Professor Kirk, Matt Lincoln, Shane Spencer, Sarah McCaffrey and Imogene Smith," he read aloud. "Am I missing anyone?"

"The instructors," I added. "My husband's partner was Paul."

"My partner was Gary, Sarah's partner was Glenn and Matt's partner was Mitchell," Imogene recounted.

"Yes, I've spoken with all four men. Mrs. Spencer, did you notice anything out of place before the jump?"

"What do you mean by out of place?" I questioned. "As far as I could tell, everyone was busy reviewing the safety videos and getting acquainted with their instructors."

"Did you notice any suspicious activity?" Detective Kane continued grilling us.

"Suspicious activity? Like what?" Imogene asked obviously agitated.

"Did you witness any strangers or even a member of the skydiving center around the packs?"

"The packs? The packs underwent a safety check twice and they were placed in the airplane hangar," Imogene recalled. "I don't remember seeing anyone around the packs but then again, I was in the locker room for a few minutes and then visited with my friends before the jump."

"I'm assuming there was a problem with the professor's pack since his parachute didn't open," I guessed. "He'd been showing my friend, Cassandra Reynolds, his AAD device, the gadget that should have automatically opened his chute."

"So, his AAD device was working," Detective Kane jotted down in his notebook.

"I'm assuming it was since he was showing Cassandra how it worked," I answered. "Why didn't his parachute open?"

"Parachutes, as in two," he corrected me. "They didn't open because the cords were cut on both chutes. His death was intentional." He looked around at each of us as if he were gauging our reactions.

"Oh, no!" Imogene gasped and covered her open mouth with her hand. "Who would want the professor dead?"

"That's what I intend to find out," Detective Kane said solemnly. "Thank you for your information and I'm sure I'll be in touch soon with more questions," he said as he rose to leave.

"Thank you detective," I said and got up to escort him to the door.

"Here's my card," he said handing it to me. "If there's anything you recall, no matter how insignificant, please call me. I'm going to need to interview Ms. McCaffrey, Mr. Lincoln and Mr. Spencer when they're available. I'll be in touch."

"Yes, of course," Imogene promised as we shut the door firmly behind him.

"This was intentional!" Lucy exclaimed. "Who in their right mind would want to kill Jonathan Kirk?"

"Someone who's out of their mind," I quickly retorted. Who could have a possible motive to kill the professor? Was there a personal problem between Jonathan Kirk and someone at the skydiving center? Paul told us he had been jumping with him for years. Maybe there was a backstory to the professor? After all, my sixth sense had told me to proceed with caution when I first met him. I find it's always best to listen to that "little voice."

❧    ❧    ❧

"What a nice turnout," Imogene commented as we scrambled to find a seat. There must have been more than five hundred people packed into the auditorium. There was an assortment of costumed characters, mourners dressed in black attire and the media who had turned out in full force to cover the memorial.

"What an interesting congregation," Lucy muttered as she angled her eyes towards the person seated adjacent to her. The woman was wearing an alien costume straight off the screen of *Close Encounters of the Third Kind*. It was difficult to act as though this were normal attire for a memorial.

"Jonathan would've been pleased with the number of people who came to pay their respects," Sarah wept as she removed her glasses and dabbed her bloodshot eyes. "He had so many admirers."

"More like mutants," Olivia whispered in my ear as she looked around the room. "Why are these people dressed for Halloween instead of a memorial?"

"Liv, don't make me laugh," I hushed her as I noticed a man costumed as Chewbacca enter the auditorium.

"What are you two giggling about?" Matt leaned over and asked.

"Not a thing. I'm having a *Star Wars* flashback," Olivia explained. "It seems irreverent to wear a costume."

"These are Jonathan's fans," Sarah spoke up. "These are

the people who supported his work and appreciated his books."

"How are you doing, dear?" Lucy put her arm around Sarah and gave her a supportive squeeze. None of us intentionally wanted to upset her.

"I'm hanging in there," Sarah said and gave a feeble smile. "I'm blessed I was able to meet Jonathan and connect with him. He'll continue to live on in the hearts of his readers."

The lights were lowered in the seating area as the stage lights were bumped up. A man in a shiny dark suit with slicked back hair approached the podium on stage and looked somberly around the audience. He paused dramatically for a minute to allow the crowd to find their seats.

"Hello, I'm King O'Conner," he introduced himself into the microphone. "I was Jonathan Kirk's manager, but privileged to call him friend for nearly twenty years. Like many of you, I'm at a loss for words to describe the grief I'm feeling. The world has lost not only a prolific author, but a tremendous scholar and exceptional teacher. I'd like to ask each of you to please join me in a moment of silence to remember our dear friend, Jonathan Kirk."

He bowed his head and closed his eyes. The auditorium was eerily quiet as everyone observed a moment of silence. More than a few people could be heard sniffling and crying. No one moved as the seconds clicked on the clock.

"Thank you. And now I'd like to invite you to watch this photo montage we've put together in Jonathan's honor," he said and exited the stage.

"Who was that?" Olivia leaned across and asked Sarah.

"That was King O'Conner, Jonathan's manager. I

met him at Jonathan's book signing the other day," she explained.

The screen faded to black as a video of Professor Kirk appeared speaking to a packed lecture hall of students. He was describing the definition of paranormal psychology and asked a volunteer to come forward to demonstrate a guessing game using a deck of cards. He was extremely animated and it was apparent he enjoyed teaching.

"I can't believe he's gone," Sarah cried and buried her face in Lucy's shoulder. "I know he's here with us. I can sense his presence in this room."

"This is precisely what I feared," Olivia whispered. She's been telling Lucy and Imogene she thinks Jonathan hasn't crossed over and he's stuck between two dimensions."

"What?" I said disbelieving. Oh dear. Sarah was hopeful she could continue communication with Jonathan.

"Of course she's going to want that," Olivia reasoned. "He wrote the text book on the theory of two dimensions. Sarah thinks he has unresolved business and she's the channel to guide him."

"He does have unresolved business. Someone sabotaged both his parachutes, remember?" I reminded her.

"Chances are that person is here at this memorial," Lincoln joined in the whispered discussion.

"Why would you think that?" I asked bewildered.

"It's a pattern I've noticed from my years in the force. The murderer habitually turns up at the scene of the crime or attends the funeral. It could because of overpowering guilt or a sick thrill because they got away with it," Matt speculated.

"That's revolting," Olivia spoke up.

"Whoever cut both his chutes is dangerous," I mumbled.

The screen continued showing one picture fading into another as the collage showed Professor Kirk at book signings, posing with fans, skydiving with his club in New Mexico and smiling with students. It was a touching tribute.

"Is that why the cops are everywhere? They're looking for the sick-o who did this?" Olivia presumed.

I surveyed the room searching for anyone who looked suspicious or guilty. Unfortunately it would be easy to camouflage one's self in this crowd.

"I'm sure they're following leads," Lincoln speculated.

"You know something, don't you?" Olivia turned and confronted her husband.

"Let's not go there. You know I can't talk about police business," he answered.

"Just as I thought, you do," Olivia whispered angrily. "You cops are thicker than thieves when it comes to protecting each other. If you haven't forgotten, we all witnessed his death. I think we've a right to know what happened to the professor. There's a murderer on the loose."

"Simmer down, Liv, and pay attention to the service," I said in a hushed warning. People were beginning to turn around to see who was talking. I smiled politely at them and prayed she'd be quiet.

The memorial continued without any further disruptions from our group. Several of Jonathan's peers spoke about his friendship and how much they admired him as a writer and researcher. Many of the speakers were well-known sci-fi authors and I was impressed with how highly he was regarded. I had to rethink my original assessment of the professor and ask myself if I'd been overly judgmental because I was a skeptic or had I assumed he was a phony because I was uncomfortable with the subject matter? I had have to give him credit for treating Sarah well in the short time they'd known each other.

"That was very moving," Imogene reflected as she blew her nose and took out her compact to touch up her makeup.

"He'll be missed," Lucy added and patted Sarah on her back.

"I would like to offer my condolences to King," Sarah told us. She motioned towards the tall man who'd introduced the montage.

"Would you like us to come with you?" Cassandra offered.

"I'd appreciate it. That would be nice," she agreed. "I'd like to introduce everyone to him," she said moving towards King O'Conner. A tall statuesque brunette in her mid-forties stood next to him. Her mascara was smeared around her eyes. I noticed she glared at Sarah before she replaced her dark Giorgio Armani sunglasses. Her tight fitting wrap dress barely contained her enormous bosoms. She reminded me of a playmate past her prime suffering from an addiction to plastic surgery.

"Why is that woman staring at Sarah?" Olivia asked grabbing my arm.

I had noticed her stiffen as Sarah approached and I stood back and observed the scene as it played out. Whoever she was, it was obvious she felt threatened by our meek friend.

"Hello, King." Sarah greeted the manager and shook his hand. "I'm Sarah McCaffrey. We met at Jonathan's book signing a few days ago. I'm devastated by loss. I know you must be as well."

"Jonathan and I had a long history. I'll miss him tremendously," he said somberly smoothing the lapels of his black Italian suit.

"These are my good friends from Dogwood Cove," Sarah said and introduced us, "Shane and Amelia Spencer, Cassandra Reynolds, Imogene Smith, Lucy Lyle, and Matt and Olivia Lincoln. This is King O'Conner, Jonathan's manager."

"Hello and thank you for coming. It's my understanding you were the skydiving party that accompanied Jonathan. What a tragedy!"

"Yes, yes it was," Imogene agreed. "We're all shocked."

"I'm so sorry for your loss Mr. O'Conner," Cassandra said politely shaking his hand covering it with her free hand in a comforting gesture. "I know the professor was extremely excited about his book tour," she said shaking her head sadly.

"We'll have to carry on in his memory," King said brushing a strand of his slicked black hair out of his eyes. "He was a talented author and this book will be his breakout best seller. It deserves my full attention."

The brunette accompanying King looked around and impatiently. She tapped her stilettoes and pursed in lips in obvious annoyance. I assumed our company must be boring her. In my book of southern manners, she was behaving rudely.

"Oh, I'm sorry," King suddenly became aware of his disgruntled companion. "This is Sloan Kirk, Jonathan's first wife," he announced.

Was there a second wife? I hoped not. Did Sarah realize Jonathan had been married?

"Hello," she said aloofly. She adjusted the collar of her mink jacket and continued staring coldly in Sarah's direction.

"It's nice to meet you," I responded politely and extended my hand. She took a step back and looked away. I smiled as I cast a puzzled look at my friends. What was her problem? Maybe she was an "alpha female" who didn't like competition from other women, even if it was at a memorial service.

"Sloan and I are committed to sharing Jonathan's book with the world. We'll press on and continue the book tour with a heavy heart," he said turning towards her for verification. He took her heavily festooned hand in a demonstrative show of a united front. She abruptly pulled free and rushed away.

"I'm sorry. Sloan is heartbroken over Jonathan's death. She's not herself at all," he apologized clearly annoyed with her behavior as a flush rose up his neck.

"Obviously," Olivia commented under her breath.

"Bless her heart," Sarah declared as she looked sympathetically at King. "You need to go after her and make sure she's alright," she urged him.

"You're right. Excuse me." He adjusted his tie and looked embarrassed as he strode off after her.

"What an odd woman," Olivia observed and took her husband's arm. "She reminds me a bit of Alexis Carrington with her uppity attitude, designer duds and mink jacket. Who still wears fur these days? It's politically incorrect."

"Alexis Carrington? Should I know who that is?" Matt asked confused.

"*Dynasty,* darling!" Imogene informed him as she imitated a British accent. "Don't tell me you can't remember the famous cat fights between Alexis and Crystal? I wonder if the former Mrs. Kirk's mink stole was real or faux?"

"I remember the gigantic shoulder pads," Lucy piped up. "Yes that woman acted oddly. I'm betting her coat was the real deal. It's such a shame killing innocent animals for fashion. You won't catch me in fur."

"She's grieving," Sarah said taking up for her. "I'm sure she was close to Jonathan at one time.'"

"How close is what I want to know," Olivia deduced. "If looks could kill, you'd be dead by now Sarah. Did he tell you he'd been married before?"

"Why would she have a problem with me? I've never met her," Sarah said aghast. "And yes, I was aware Jonathan had been married. He and Sloan divorced almost four years ago."

"Don't be naïve, Sarah! She was throwing daggers at you from behind those gigantic designer shades," Olivia informed her.

"Go easy, Liv," Matt advised his wife. "Maybe she's mad at King O'Conner and we interrupted a disagreement?"

"I'm over-ruling you on this one, Lincoln," Cassandra disagreed. "My radar is on full alert. That woman was openly glowering at Sarah. My intuition's telling me there's much more to Sloan Kirk than a grieving ex-wife."

"Sounds like a man," Imogene said knowingly as she put her hand on her hip.

"Everything sounds like a man to you," Lucy ribbed her.

"You're right Imogene," Cassandra agreed. "She still had

feelings for Jonathan and she didn't like the recent attention he lavished on Sarah."

"You can't be serious Cassandra? You think the professor still had something going on with that dragon queen? I'm having a hard time picturing them married," Olivia commented. "He had that hippie ponytail and three-piece suit-thing going on while she's so artificial looking with her over-the-hill *Baywatch* babe body."

"I'm not saying they were involved," Cassandra said trying to hit rewind as she saw the hurt on Sarah's face, "what I'm saying is she had designs on him and you interfered with her plans."

"How do you know all this?" Shane asked bewildered. "Do you read tarot cards now?"

"Shane, honey, it doesn't take a tarot card reader or psychic to recognize a scorned woman."

"That reminds me of my second marriage to Stan," Imogene interjected.

"Good grief, here she goes again," Lucy said in mild disapproval.

"Do you mind, Lucy? Our young friend Sarah is need of some womanly advice. Now where was I?" she asked and shot an annoyed look in Lucy's direction.

"Husband number two, Stan," Lincoln reminded her and chuckled. "Shane, I think we need a stiff drink. Want to find the bar?"

"Good idea. Ladies, we'll be back!" he smiled and looked relieved. The poor guys had too much estrogen swirling around them. I didn't blame them for ducking us for a while.

"Stan was the love of my life. He was dashing, charming,

handsome in a George Clooney kind of way, and he attracted all kinds of female attention without trying," she reminisced as he eyes misted. "We had that passionate kind of love that happens only once in a lifetime."

"Liz Taylor had that kind of passion several times as I recall," Lucy joked.

"I'm talking about love, not lust. Don't confuse the two," Imogene corrected her.

"He sounds perfect. What happened?" Sarah asked with wide eyes.

"He cheated on her, that's what happened," Olivia predicted.

"No, he died," Imogene said sadly and looked down at the floor. It was obvious she still missed him terribly.

"How is Stan like Jonathan? I thought you were convinced Sloan Kirk still had feelings for him?" Olivia asked confused.

"Oh she does. She reminds me of Stan's young sexy secretary, the one who tried to seduce him," Imogene vividly remembered. "When Stan didn't respond to her advances, she became bitter and decided she would try to ruin our marriage by informing me she was having an affair with my husband."

"I never knew this about Uncle Stan," I said shocked. "What happened?"

"I confronted him and recapped the conversation. I'd packed up everything and told him I was leaving. He was so hurt. I wish I'd never had that conversation with him," she revealed. "His secretary later confessed to me she had concocted the entire story because she he ignored her advances."

"You had to know the truth. I'd want to know," Olivia spoke up. "If I thought Lincoln was cheating, I'd go berserk!"

"You think you would, but when wounds go deep, sometimes you handle it differently than you imagined," Cassandra admitted.

"But what happened with Uncle Stan?" I brought the conversation back around. I always remembered them being such a happy couple at our family holidays and get-togethers.

"He was hurt that I didn't trust him and it caused a rift between us. He eventually forgave me and I think it made us much closer. I learned a valuable lesson. I never took my husband for granted again," Imogene declared.

"And so what about Jonathan reminds you of Stan?" Lucy probed.

"I can recognize a rebuked woman. Sloan Kirk didn't get what she wanted and she's become jealous of Sarah. Don't let that plasticized socialite take your happy memories with the professor away from you," Imogene said giving Sarah a long hug. "He had feelings for you, I'm sure of it."

"Don't look now but dragon lady is coming this way," Olivia warned as we braced ourselves for her fury.

"Jonathan loved me," she said through clenched teeth as she confronted Sarah. "I was the one woman in his life that satisfied him. You were nothing but one of his dalliances, another fawning fan. You couldn't possibly have made Jonathan happy!" she yelled and threw her drink in Sarah's face.

"What's going on here?" King O'Conner rushed up behind the crazed woman and grabbed her arm as she lunged towards Sarah, ready to take the assault to the next level. He held both of her arms behind her back as she kicked at Sarah.

"You're psychotic busty friend here threw her drink in Sarah's face," Olivia informed him. She gathered all five feet of herself and stood toe-to-toe with Sloan Kirk. "You'd better get her out of here before we press charges. My husband is an officer of the law and one word from Sarah and you'll be spending the night in the slammer!"

"Sloan, get a hold of yourself! Have you been drinking again?" he accused the misbehaving woman.

"She ruined everything, all *our* plans!" she screamed as the room became awkwardly quiet and everyone turned their attention towards the chaos.

"What's going on here?" Matt Lincoln reappeared and stood between the two women.

"She came across the room and threw a drink in my face," Sarah told him as she took a napkin and dabbed her face. "She's crazy! And to think I felt sorry for you."

"Sorry for me? You're so pathetic!" Sloan laughed nastily. "Jonathan toyed with you like he did all his little 'Kirk worshippers.' One more day and he would have dumped you like he did all the others."

"Get her out of here and sober her up," Lincoln growled at King O'Conner. "Sarah, are you OK?" he said turning his attention toward the trembling woman.

"I'm fine. I'd like to leave and get a fresh change of clothes," she told us. "I appreciate your support, but I think we've worn out our welcome."

Indeed we had worn out our welcome. But Sarah's problems with the former Mrs. Kirk were only starting.

# CHAPTER TEN

"What was that all about?" Olivia asked pacing back and forth in our suite. Sarah was showering and then we'd go out for dinner. Imogene and Cassandra were sitting on the sofa looking out the window at the Vegas skyline.

"It could have been the booze talking or she is certifiable," Cassandra declared. "Either way, she's an evil woman taking her anger out on Sarah like that."

"It's strange how hateful people have such similar characteristics," I said referring to our run-in with Dixie Beauregard's killer who almost cost our lives. "It's as if they subscribe to the same book of phraseology and use it to inflict the greatest collateral damage."

"I couldn't agree more. I've called Detective Kane to report what happened. I think he'll take a closer look at Sloan Kirk. She sounds like someone with a motive to cut those parachute cords," Matt Lincoln stated.

"Do you really believe she'd do something that vindictive?" I asked in disbelief.

"The ex-spouse is the first person the police suspect," Matt answered. "If she was in Vegas yesterday, she better have an airtight alibi."

"She's a venomous creature," Imogene commented. "I don't know her from Adam, but I can't imagine a marriage with her would've been a walk in the park. The professor probably ran all the way to the courthouse to get away from her."

"I wouldn't be so sure. Isn't it obvious why the professor would want a woman like that? It's all about the physical. It makes me sick how men will throw themselves at a woman just because her chest's inflated like two beach balls. Is that attractive to you, Lincoln?" Olivia probed.

"Don't answer that," Imogene intervened. "It's a set-up and you're screwed either way."

"What do you mean?" he asked in mocked innocence.

"If you say you prefer a natural woman, Olivia will think you're pacifying her," Shane expertly explained. "If you say breast size doesn't matter, she'll accuse you of lying. If you admit you prefer a bit more cleavage, you will never hear the end of it. So my advice is to say N O T H I N G!"

"Sounds like you should have taken your own advice," I teased him and hit him with a sofa throw pillow. "Shane's right. Some topics are bound to lead to an argument. It's best to avoid the controversy in the first place."

"I'll have you know that I am one hundred percent all natural," Imogene crowed and jumped up to parade around the room swaying her ample hips. "I've never injected fillers, Botox, or put silicone in this body!"

"Back to the 'black widow,'" Cassandra interrupted the

sideshow. "I'm concerned for Sarah's safety. That woman would have hurt her if King and Lincoln hadn't intervened."

"It would never go that far. She didn't stand a chance against me," Olivia said boldly.

"And what exactly would you have done to her?" Cassandra snickered.

"I'd have her down on the ground hogtied in eight seconds flat just like my calves," Olivia proudly declared. "And don't think I wouldn't do it. I'd love to hear what she'd say then."

"I'd like to know what plans Sarah ruined. Didn't y'all think it was odd for her to say that?" I posed to the group.

"She was drunk. Who knows what she meant?" Shane speculated. "Maybe she was trying to get back together with Jonathan and he told her about Sarah."

"What about the things she said to Sarah about being another of the professor's conquests? She doesn't need to hear trash talk like that about a man who is no longer here to defend himself or their relationship," Imogene said with concern. "That's like a dagger to the heart for that girl."

"I agree. Sarah didn't know Jonathan long enough to know much about him. Anyone could say anything at this point and it could destroy his credibility with her," I said.

"The police will be thoroughly investigating Professor Kirk's background. If he had any skeletons in the closet, they'll find them. I'd guess they've already interviewed the staff at his school in New Mexico. I'll call Keith Kane and see what he's willing to share," Matt said and rose to walk to the bedroom for privacy.

"If he finds out something, I'm not sure we should tell

Sarah," Olivia thought out loud. "I'm not sure she can handle more bad news."

"I can't handle what?" Sarah questioned as entered the suite with Lucy in tow.

"We were discussing what happened," Imogene quickly spoke up. "I'm hoping what that scourge of a woman said about Jonathan doesn't take away from what you shared with him."

"I've never been treated like that and I admit she did shake me up, but I'm fine now," Sarah said forcefully. "You don't need to worry about me. I'm a strong person."

"Yes you are and you've got your friends to support you," Cassandra said.

"I just got off the phone with Keith Kane," Lincoln said re-entering the living room. "He's on his way over with some information he'd like to discuss with us."

"What is it? I'm sure he told you," Olivia pushed.

"He was evasive," Lincoln told her. "I have no idea but he wanted to make sure Sarah would be here."

"Well, there go the dinner plans," Olivia said deflated. "Maybe we should call room service and order some appetizers if this is going to take a while."

"Can you think of anything other than your stomach?" Cassandra said with displeasure. "Poor Sarah is going through this terrible ordeal and you're more concerned with buffalo wings and quesadillas."

"Actually, that sounds good," Olivia said as she picked up the room service menu. "They also have goat cheese and crackers with assorted fruit. I definitely could go for that."

"Does she even realize how she acts?" Cassandra was

annoyed, but I was glad to see her back with our tea ladies. "Matt, snap some sense into her!"

"Hey, I've got to keep my wits sharp about me now and I can feel the blood sugar level tanking. What does everyone else want?"

"I didn't eat lunch so appetizers sound good," Sarah said easing the situation. "Liv doesn't mean any harm. She's a woman driven by a high metabolism."

"You're always thoughtful, Sarah McCaffrey," I grinned watching the antics between my close friends. We certainly were an eclectic bunch of personalities.

We placed an order and waited for the detective. A few minutes later, Keith Kane arrived and Lincoln ushered him in.

"Keith," he said shaking his hand and leading him to the seating area. "You said you had some questions for Sarah?"

"I do. Miss. McCaffrey, I thought you might be more comfortable answering questions here instead of the station," he suggested.

"I'm more than happy to help in anyway. What did you want to know?" Sarah inquired curiously.

"Why did you mention going to the station?" Olivia interrupted. "Is she under investigation for some reason?" she confronted the detective.

"We've been given information that you were the last person seen with Mr. Kirk's manuscript for his next book. That manuscript has been reported missing. Do you have it?"

"I'm confused. What does a manuscript have to do with someone sabotaging his parachutes? I think you're barking up the wrong tree," Imogene commented.

"Everyone, settle down and let Sarah answer the question," Matt Lincoln encouraged the overprotective group of women. "This is routine questioning, right Keith?"

"I'm following up on the possibility this manuscript's disappearance may have had something to do with his death," the investigator reasoned. "We don't know that's why we're asking the questions. Do you have expertise in this area that would allow you to make a credible claim for authorship?"

"I did have Jonathan's manuscript for *Bridging the Transition A Ghost's Guide to the After Life,*" Sarah nodded. "He invited me to his room the evening we went to dinner and the 'O' show. He was elated he'd finished his next novel and wanted me to read it. I don't have it now. I returned it to him," she calmly explained.

"You don't have it? Are you sure?" Detective Kane probed.

"I told you, I don't have it. You think I stole his manuscript? Why would I do that?" she asked flabbergasted.

"For personal gain," he replied. "With the professor out of the way, you could claim to be the author and publish the book."

"What? That's ridiculous!" Lucy interjected. "Who in their right mind would think Sarah would do such a thing? Killing a man to publish a book is ludicrous!"

"Jonathan asked me to review the book as a favor to him. He wanted to know my honest opinion because I've collected every volume he's ever written," Sarah told the policeman.

"How do you know someone else didn't take the book," Olivia pointed out, "maybe a housekeeper or bellman from his hotel? Could it be locked in the safe of his room?"

"We have video of Miss McCaffrey leaving the professor's room carrying the manuscript. You were the last person seen with it," he indicated.

"I gave it back to him the next day when we went skydiving," Sarah offered. "The reason I was so tired and wanted coffee that morning was because I'd been up all night reading his book. I made a point of returning it quickly because he was going to pitch it to a major publisher attending Comic Con."

"I wonder who the publisher was. Did he say?" Cassandra inquired.

"And of course, conveniently there is no video of her giving it back to him," Olivia surmised. "Who told you the manuscript was missing?"

"A Mrs. Sloan Kirk," the detective read from his notebook. "She reported the manuscript missing yesterday morning."

"Sloan Kirk as in Jonathan's ex-wife?" Lucy asked incredulously. "Why would she be trying to get her hands on his manuscript? That in itself is suspicious," she said acerbically.

"Jonathan and Sloan weren't close," Sarah shared with the officer. "I don't believe he would've wanted Sloan benefitting from his next book."

"And what makes you say that?" Keith Kane pried and leaned back waiting for an explanation.

"He told me he was emotionally and financially devastated by their divorce," she said. "He told me he'd finally overcome writer's block, which he claimed was a direct result of their stressful marriage," Sarah clarified. "It doesn't make sense for her to have anything to do with his book.

According to Jonathan, they weren't on speaking terms."

"This is the same Sloan Kirk who threw a drink in Sarah's face at his memorial service today. Did you have cameras capturing that?" Olivia asked sarcastically. "And you don't think it's a coincidence that she reported the manuscript was missing? I'm assuming she must have gone through his hotel room to search for it after his death. Was she an invited guest or did she break into his room?"

"We're looking into that," Detective Kane answered uneasily. I don't think he was accustomed to being addressed like that during a questioning. His mood appeared to be darkening.

"Why was Sloan in Las Vegas to begin with?" Imogene remarked. "Did she fly in for the service or was she stalking the professor?"

"Mrs. Kirk was attending Comic Con as a guest," the officer informed us.

"A guest of whom may I ask?" Cassandra inquired approaching the officer. She straightened her jacket and looked him squarely in the eye. I knew that determined face from the boardroom. She smelled blood in the water and wasn't backing down.

"She's attending Comic Con as a guest of King O'Conner," Keith Kane revealed.

"King O'Conner, Jonathan's manager?" Sarah asked stunned. "King O'Conner invited her to Comic Con knowing the contentious feelings between Jonathan and Sloan? Why would he do that?"

"Sarah, I think we may have discovered there's more to what we witnessed than Jonathan's ex-wife showing up at the last minute. It appears those two had something going on right under the professor's nose," Cassandra submitted. "They appeared to be arguing when Sarah introduced everyone."

"Lover's quarrel," Imogene deduced. "The body language spoke volumes. She was angry with him."

"And drunk," Lucy agreed. "It's no wonder she was so nasty to you Sarah. She wanted Jonathan back and she knew his next book would be a best seller. She wanted a piece of the action and she'd have a lot of explaining to do if she were sleeping with King O'Conner. Their affair could ruin everything!"

"She probably thought she could waltz back into his life, push up her big ta tas and win him back. She wasn't betting on you," Olivia concluded.

"Wait a minute, hold on!" Shane interrupted. "How can you be sure this is true? Who says because she was a guest of King O'Conner that she is involved with him? Maybe they're close friends."

"I love you Shane, but I'll wager her guest accommodations are the same room number as King's," I speculated.

"Let's not jump to conclusions until the detective completes his investigation," Shane recommended.

"Sure and let's watch Sarah get railroaded into becoming 'suspect number one' on a short list," Olivia reproved him as she pushed her red curls out of her face. She was getting fired up.

"You know I don't want that," Shane retorted. "Don't put words in my mouth, Liv."

"Time out everyone," I announced. "We're forgetting a

crucial fact. What happened to the manuscript? Sarah said she gave it back to the professor. Was it at the hotel?"

"No, he picked me up and I had it in my overnight bag. I brought a change of clothes with me because we had planned to go out to dinner after the jump," she clarified.

"What did he do with it?" Cassandra impatiently asked.

"He put it inside his duffle bag and we drove over to the skydiving center. I don't know what happened to it after that," she confessed.

"The manuscript was not among his personal effects," Keith Kane disclosed. "The duffle bag was in his locker, but no book."

"Someone took it!" Cassandra shouted. "I bet it's the same person who cut his parachute cords."

If Cassandra's hunch were true, his murder was premeditated for the sole purpose of financial gain. If the professor's prediction was accurate and his current book and the sequel soared on *The New York Times* best sellers and were translated into film, there was a fortune to be made. Who would benefit the most from the professor's death? His ex-wife was a possibility depending on their divorce agreement. King O'Conner, his manager of over twenty years, was quickly climbing to the top of my suspect list. The police would conduct their own investigation but we needed to research all avenues and get to the bottom of this immediately.

# CHAPTER ELEVEN

"You don't think King will be the least bit suspicious?" Lucy asked as she awkwardly adjusted her costume. "I feel ridiculous, like a kid dressed up for trick or treating."

"No one will know it's us and that's the point of wearing these getups," Imogene answered her roommate. "I just wish they had the *I Dream of Jeannie* costume in my size instead of these ugly tunics. Dressing like a Klingon is not what I had in mind."

"That's the point, we're trying to blend in with everyone at Comic Con," Olivia said. "This is the only way we can get close enough to observe King without him realizing we're right in front of him."

"You should have warned me these things were made out of polyester. I've scratched so much, I think I have hives," Cassandra moaned.

"Lincoln will kill me if he finds out we did this," Olivia said muffled under her rubber mask. "He told me the best way to help Sarah was to let the police proceede with their investigation and keep my nose clean."

"We're not interfering. We're doing our own undercover surveillance," I laughed as we walked into the main corridor. "I'm thankful this place has air conditioning because I'm already burning up. How do the actors manage to work without melting under the hot studio lights?" I whined as I attempted to take another sip of water through a straw. I was slowly getting used to drinking through the mouth hole of the mask.

"I don't think the boys will suspect a thing. They were too eager to go play golf. We just need to remember to get these costumes back before the store closes at nine," I reminded myself.

"Tell Sarah to slow down. I can hardly see a thing," Imogene called ahead to Lucy as I grabbed her arm to assist her. "I can't walk in these combat boots. They're too clunky."

"You can manage stilettos without a problem. These might take some getting used to," I reassured her as we walked through the crowded aisles.

"Stop, they're handing out free samples of space food," Olivia called out and moved closer to a table with an assortment of freeze dried products.

"Don't eat that garbage," Cassandra warned her. "You don't know how old it is. Keep up!"

"That's the point. Its freeze dried. It doesn't go bad," Olivia argued.

"And my point is you'll eat anything, even if it has no taste at all," Cassandra responded angrily. "We're here for information gathering, not sampling."

"He's over there at Jonathan's booth," Sarah pointed as

we huddled together to strategize. He was standing and talking with a young man in his late twenties. They appeared to be having an animated conversation. "What should we do now?"

"Try and look natural," Cassandra suggested. "Let's see if we can get a bit closer to overhear what they're discussing."

"I wonder how do you look natural dressed like a character from *Star Trek*?" Lucy whispered loudly.

"Think like a Klingon and you'll blend in," Imogene coached, "and stop worrying. No one here has even given us a second look."

We casually moved across the aisle and made our way towards Jonathan's booth. A large sign bearing his photograph was displayed on an easel. The words "greatly missed but never forgotten" were imprinted across the top. The fans had made a makeshift memorial of mounded flowers..

"I'm trying my best not to cry," Sarah confessed as she looked at the touching tribute. "I've got to help find out who did this to Jonathan. He'd want me to bring his killer to justice."

"He'd want the police to bring him to justice," I corrected her. "He'd want you to know the truth, but not risk your safety."

"Of course he'd want that. I'm trying to explain that I feel a connection with him s as though he's here with me, he's guiding me. I don't know how else to express it," Sarah concluded.

"There, there my sweetheart," Imogene soothed and placed her arm around her. "Of course you still feel a connection with the professor. We all do."

"No, not like this, Imogene. This is different. I have a sense that Jonathan's guiding me towards information," Sarah patiently explained. "I'm paying close attention to my sixth sense as he instructed in his book."

"Don't ask," Olivia told Imogene. "She's diluted her brain with that mumbo jumbo and I've about had it. If she doesn't snap out of this, I'm going to sit her down and have an intervention."

"Let's stand over here next to the Kryptonite display," I instructed my crew. It was adjacent to Jonathan's area and afforded us cover while we eavesdropped on King O'Conner's discussion, which had become increasingly louder.

"That's not what we agreed upon. I never should have listened to you and gone behind Jonathan's back," the scruffy man angrily said.

"You're a complete unknown, a novice. You think you can get printed without my help? I have years of experience and all the right contacts. You can't get this book in front of a major publisher without me." King proclaimed shaking his finger in the younger man's face.

"You're forgetting you need *me*," the fledgling author reminded the pompous manager. "You can't peddle this book as your creation. I was Jonathan's research assistant. It's expected I'd to pick up his torch and carry on."

"There are a thousand newbie writers waiting to cut their teeth on this garbage. You'll do exactly as I tell you or the deal is off," King threatened standing toe-to-toe with the unidentified man. "I can easily find someone else. Don't underestimate me," he sneered.

"I think you're the one doing the underestimating. I want

fifty percent or I'll go to the press with this and don't think I won't," he avowed.

"You're out of your mind!" King sputtered. "Fifty percent is highway robbery. Let me remind you, I found you when you were schlepping drinks in that dive with no prospect of a future in writing. Who do you think you are demanding fifty percent?"

"I don't owe you a thing. The way I see it, both of you owe me," the disheveled man bellowed. "I worked my tail off on *Bridging the Transition* as well as the first book and what do I have to show for it? Jonathan wasn't even generous enough to give me any credit."

"You were hired as a ghost writer and you were paid handsomely. Why do you think you deserve to have your name on the cover?" King O'Conner spoke up.

"Because I'm that good! Jonathan Kirk was a washed up 'has been.' All the success the first book received is because of me!" he bragged. "Don't push me, King or I'll go straight to *Skeptics Magazine* and blow the roof off your book and movie deal!"

"You wouldn't dare!" King glowered.

"You need a front man for this book. I'm the only one with enough credibility. You need me as much as I need you old friend," he sneered and patted the older man on the shoulder. "You'll agree to my terms or I'll follow through with my interview with Brian Myers. And don't think of doing anything stupid. If anything happens to me Myers will be receiving a DVD with all the details spelled out. You'll be ruined and your book tour will be finished." He stormed off and left King O'Conner standing with his mouth hanging open. The older manager quickly gathered his composure and glanced around to see if anyone had witnessed the exchange.

We were standing in a tight group pretending to admire the glowing green Kryptonite rocks. I was relieved we were masked so we couldn't see the disappointment on Sarah's face. Her hero and love interest had been knocked off his pedestal. I knew she was devastated by the information we overheard.

"Let's get out of here," Olivia suggested. "I'm burning up and think I've seen enough of Comic Con to last a lifetime!"

"Let's go. I'm ready to get these boots off," Imogene agreed. "Is there somewhere we can sit down?"

"I think we need to get out of here first and then find a spot to take a break," Cassandra advised. "I don't think I can make it all the way back to the hotel in this costume. It's too hot!"

"Serendipity is right across the street," Olivia piped up. "We could go have a hot frozen chocolate and cool off there," she said hopefully.

"Wearing these outfits?" Lucy asked amazed. "What would people think of us?"

"They've seen everything from Elvis to Marilyn Monroe. I doubt anyone will pay attention," I presumed. "I think going somewhere cooler is a plan. I can't wait to ditch my mask," I said removing mine as we left the large exhibition area. I fluffed my matted hair and waved my hands in front of my face in an attempt to circulate fresh air.

"I think the coast is clear," Olivia stated and removed her mask. Beads of sweat had formed on her forehead and her thick auburn hair was wet. "Latex and polyester are not my friends. Give me breathable denim any day."

"How far is Serendipity?" Imogene inquired. "I'm going to have to take these Frankenstein shoes off and soak my feet when we get back to the hotel."

Sarah was silent as she pulled off her mask and walked across the street with us. I pulled her close and leaned my head against hers. She wiped away a tear and her face contorted in obvious pain. She'd endured so much in the past two days and I couldn't imagine what she was feeling at the moment.

"May we have a booth for six please," Cassandra requested. The hostess smiled and glanced at our costumes.

"You must be here for Comic Con," she observed. "I hope you're enjoying your visit to Las Vegas," she politely said as she led us to a large booth in the far corner.

"Thank you," I smiled as she passed out our menus. "I know what I'm having," I said decisively.

"Let me guess, a frozen hot chocolate?" Olivia accurately predicted.

"Are we ready to order?" an efficient server asked us as we glanced at our menus.

"Are we ready ladies? I know I'm having a frozen hot chocolate," I spoke up.

"That sounds cold and refreshing," Lucy agreed. "I think I will also."

"Frozen hot chocolates all around?" the server asked.

"Yes," we all nodded in agreement.

"And I'll also have the hamburger, sweet potato fries and a house salad with balsamic vinaigrette dressing on the side,"

Olivia ordered. "What? Why's everyone looking at me?"

"You aren't seriously planning to eat all that by yourself?" Cassandra asked amazed. "The frozen hot chocolate is so rich, I'm not sure I can finish it let alone a full meal big enough for a truck driver!"

"Stop needling me, mother!" Olivia retaliated. "Thanks," she told the waitperson.

"Sarah, how are you holding up?" I quietly asked as I took a long drink of ice water.

"I'm in shock. I feel like a complete fool. I took Jonathan at his word," she shared as her lower lip trembled. She dug into the pocket of her costume for a tissue but came up empty-handed.

"Here dear," Imogene said producing a tissue from her tote. "I know this must be a hard day for you."

"He lied to me about everything!" Sarah said as her voice cut off and she began to sob.

"He hired a ghost writer. Many well-known authors do that these days. That doesn't make him a liar," Cassandra cautioned.

"He's the foremost authority on paranormal activity. He shouldn't use someone to write for him. How would anyone know if the research is original?" Sarah reasoned.

"Precisely my point all along," Olivia agreed. "Who do you ask? A spirit guide?" she said with a straight face.

"You behave," Cassandra chastised.

"I've never believed in any of this hocus pocus," Olivia defended herself. "This just proves its complete nonsense."

"The only thing I ascertained from their exchange was that the young writer was hired to do research for Jonathan's books. It doesn't disprove any of the research material," I rationalized hoping to cushion the blow Sarah had received.

"It sounds as if he's planning to claim he's the author on *Bridging the Transition.* If that's the case, he may have had motive for killing Jonathan," Sarah deduced. "With Jonathan out of the picture, he could sell the manuscript to a publisher and receive credit as the author."

"You're forgetting King O'Conner's role. This was planned out," I reminded her. "They are both in on it and we need to let Keith Kane know what we overheard."

"Sarah, there's something that's been nagging me. Did Jonathan mention which publisher at Comic Con he was pitching his manuscript to?" Cassandra asked excitedly.

"He did. Let me think what he told me," she paused as she wracked her brain. "It wasn't Simon & Schuster, that's Stephen King's publisher," Sarah struggled to recall. "It might have been Bantam, but wait that's Dean Koontz."

"Think, think. Who published his last book?" Olivia reasoned.

"That's it! It was Moon Dragon press," Sarah yelped. "They had an option on his second book. Good sleuthing, Liv!"

"What should we do?" I asked the collective group.

"Enjoy our frozen hot chocolates," Olivia said in all seriousness. The server interrupted our conversation by presenting the enormous chocolate desserts. Whipped topping, chocolate shavings and maraschino cherries made us stop and admire our selections before pouncing on them.

"Let's fuel up, change into regular clothes and request a meeting with Moon Dragon press," Cassandra said decisively.

I think they may want to know what King O'Conner and this mystery ghost writer plan to do with Jonathan's manuscript. Then we pay a visit to Detective Kane."

"Agreed," Olivia stated and took a large bite of her hamburger. "Mmm. This is delicious," she said with her mouth full of food.

After returning the Klingon garb to Leo's House of Costumes, we were once again walking through the entrance of Comic Con, this time more appropriately dressed depending on who you asked. At least we were much cooler.

"Moon Dragon has a booth in the far back corner," Sarah read after reviewing a map with the layout of the exhibitors. "Are we going to lay it all out on the table or take a more subtle approach?" she wondered.

"You read the manuscript, so you're familiar with the content. Give me a brief synopsis," Cassandra probed.

"This should be interesting," Olivia rolled her eyes. "Let me get my hip boots out to stand in the horse manure."

"Ssh, Liv!" I ordered and found myself starting to get tickled. "We have to be serious right now."

"I am being serious. It's a load of …"

"Olivia Rivers Lincoln," Cassandra warned. "If you can't keep your mouth shut during this process, go run around and occupy yourself. I won't have you blowing this," Cassandra warned vehemently. "I mean it, Liv!"

"Alright, I'll zip it. No comment, I promise!" she huffed and exhaled loudly.

"Look, its Jessica Hamby from *True Blood!*" a man yelled as he pointed at Olivia. "Can I have your autograph?" he asked thrusting a paper and pen at her.

"You've got the wrong lady, friend!" Olivia diplomatically handed him back his autograph material.

"I'd know you anywhere! You're even prettier in person," he complimented her. "Look everyone, it's Jessica Hamby. Quick, take my picture, Maude!" the man ordered his stunned wife.

"Smile," she called as the camera flashed. "One more, I think your eyes were closed Herb," she told her husband. They posed for a picture and the couple thanked her.

"Who's Jessica Hamby?" Olivia asked Sarah. "I've never heard of her."

"She's a vampire on one of the hottest shows on HBO," Sarah explained. "Very pretty red head. You do look similar to her now that I think about it. The actress who plays her is Deborah Ann Woll."

"It's Jessica Hamby," another Comic Con attendee yelled out. "Jessica, Jessica, over here!"

"This is creepy," Olivia said moving away from the aisle. "I'm not Jessica," she smiled and patiently told the disappointed fan.

"You could be her twin," a kind lady told her. "You're gorgeous!"

"Thank you," Olivia grinned and blushed at the praise. "Whoever this Jessica person is, I don't mind the attention."

"I think we've figured out how to get a private audience with the head of Moon Dragon publishing," Cassandra thought aloud. "Meet our newest celebrity autobiographer, Miss Deborah Ann Woll, AKA Jessica Hamby."

"What? No way, Cassandra! I can't pretend to be an actress. What would I say if they asked me about the show?

I don't watch it! I have no clue!"

"The show is set in a small town Louisiana where vampires and humans coexist after a Japanese scientist develops synthetic blood," Sarah quickly spelled out. "Your character was once human, but was turned into a vampire to punish another vampire who was on trial with the Vampire Magister."

"Not my cup of tea," Lucy spoke up. "Give me *The Andy Griffith Show* any day! Vampires, what nonsense."

"It's actually a great show," Sarah defended the HBO series. "The cast is outstanding."

"What is a 'Vampire Magister?'" Olivia asked perplexed. "Do I even want to know?"

"You play a human turned into a vampire on a very popular show. We'll roll with it," Cassandra said jovially. "And that's the cover story we'll use to get a private meeting with Moon Dragon's editor-in-chief, Dean Jaguar. Then we'll spring the real reason on him."

"He'll be madder than a stirred up hornet's nest," Imogene claimed.

"We need to speak with him before King O'Conner signs a book deal with Moon Dragon," I pointed out. "Otherwise he may unknowingly sign a contract with a killer."

"It's a good thing you wore your black mini-skirt and leather jacket today. You're dressed like a vampire," Sarah said optimistically.

"Great, just what I wanted to hear. I look like a vampire," Olivia commented mordantly. "And what does a vampire typically wear?"

"A black cape like Bela Lugosi," Lucy said matter-of-factly. "Now he was the best *Count Dracula.*"

"Your red boots look adorable with your outfit," Cassandra proudly noted. "A bold fashion forward statement. The red lipstick really pulls the look together. I'm surprised to see you in a short skirt."

"Lincoln likes to see my legs every once in a while," Olivia confessed. "I thought he might appreciate it."

"He will and apparently, your fans are appreciating the outfit," Imogene teased as more than a few men gawked at Olivia's slender frame.

"Jessica, Jessica!" several people yelled and took her picture as we walked by.

"This is ridiculous!" Olivia said as she clenched her teeth in a forced smile.

"Give them a little wave, play the part!" Cassandra coached. "It will help you get into the role before we meet Dean."

"And remind me what I'm supposed to say," Olivia waved at the people calling out to her.

"Sarah will do the talking. She knows the show. You can handle it, can't you Sarah?" Cassandra asked confident in her ability.

"I'm not good at lying," Sarah reminded us. "I bumble, get tongue tied, and it goes against my core beliefs as a human being."

"Get over it! Do you want to help the professor or not?" Olivia challenged her. "I'm not exactly comfortable pretending to be a blood sucking fanged monster, but I'm willing to do it if it helps find who killed Jonathan.

Sometimes you have to put your moral compass aside for the higher good."

"I'll do it," I said surprising myself. "If I can carry on a civilized conversation with Sally Stokes with a smile pasted on when I'd rather strangle her, I can wing this!"

"It's decided!" Cassandra said triumphantly. "Amelia, you're Olivia's, I mean Deborah Ann Wall's agent representing a possible book deal. The rest of us are her manager, personal assistant, stylist, makeup artist… you get the idea."

"What's my name?"

"What do you mean?" Cassandra asked.

"My agent name. I can't use my real name in case I blow it," I worried.

"You're not going to blow it," Imogene reassured me. "How about Barbara Blakenship. That sounds 'agenty.'"

"Or Suzanne Shipley. That has a nice ring," Lucy brainstormed.

"Keep it simple so you'll have no trouble letting it roll off your tongue. What about Amelia Adams. It's easy to remember," Cassandra devised.

"I can remember that," I said feeling my adrenaline rush. "Let's do this before I chicken out."

"Put these sunglasses on," Imogene instructed Olivia as she handed her a large pair of dark frames. "They're designer knock-offs. They'll never know unless they realize the 'C's' are backwards."

"Let's hope they don't," Olivia said slipping them on.

We made our way to the far back corner and found the marketing director for Moon Dragon Publishing. I quickly introduced myself and my celebrity client and patiently waited as the excitable young lady placed a call to the company president.

"Ms. Adams, I'd like you to meet Dean Jaguar, the president of Moon Dragon Publishing," the marketing director enthusiastically introduced us.

"Ms. Adams, so very nice to meet you," Dean smiled and firmly shook my hand. "And this must be Miss Woll, it's a true pleasure," he said gushing over Olivia.

"Likewise," Olivia answered and remained aloof. Perfect role playing.

"Mr. Jaguar, my client is interested in writing an autobiography based on her experience playing a modern day vampire on *True Blood*. It would also offer an all access glimpse behind the scenes of the show. With the success *Twilight* and other recent sci-fi movies have had, I think this would be an amazing project."

"Please, call me Dean," he insisted. "I couldn't agree with you more. *True Blood* has had phenomenal success. A book based on your life would have fans standing in line for their personal copy," Dean insisted. He looked pleased like the cat that caught the canary. I knew he was seeing dollar signs and would be eager to discuss a deal.

"Of course, we would maintain the rights to any and all movie options, apparel licensing, the standard contract," Cassandra spoke up.

"This is Barbara Blakenship, Miss Woll's manager," I said off the top of my head.

"Yes, of course Ms. Blakenship. We can have our attorneys draw up an agreement stating those provisions," he said agreeably. "But I'd like to hear more from Miss Woll herself. What made you decide to write an autobiography?"

I quickly looked over at Olivia who began to nervously laugh.

"Deborah is an introvert," Sarah quickly improvised. "She expresses herself best through her journaling."

"And you are?" he asked extending his hand.

"Suzanne Shipley, Deborah's personal assistant," Sarah said taking his hand. "It's a pleasure to meet such a renowned publisher. I'm a fan of your work."

"Really, that's wonderful. What work in particular are you referring to?" Dean Jaguar asked as Sarah stroked his ego.

"Jonathan Kirk's book, *A Ghost's Guide to Understanding the Modern World,*" she said proudly. "It was by far his best book to date.

"I couldn't agree with you more. What a loss we are feeling at Moon Dragon. Jonathan was one of our most popular authors. I'm not sure anyone can fill his shoes," the publisher said sincerely.

"I'd like to speak with you about Mr. Kirk's works," I said looking directly into the man's eyes. "We have information pertaining to his second manuscript, *Bridging the Transition.*

"What do you ladies know about Jonathan Kirk's manuscript? Is this some kind of joke?" he said sensing he'd been misled. He began to look intently in Olivia's direction. I knew the jig was up. We'd better wrap it up!

"Dean, we're not here to talk with you about a book deal for Deborah Ann Woll," Cassandra admitted. "We have information that Jonathan Kirk used a ghost writer on his last two books. Were you aware of that?" Cassandra asked pointedly.

"Who are you?" he demanded.

"We're friends of Jonathan's and we were with him when he died," Sarah explained stepping forward. "We're trying to help the police find his murderer. We have information from a reliable source that Jonathan may have been killed for the rights to his books."

"I think it would be best if you left whoever you are," Dean Jaguar exploded. "You've wasted my time with your games. Patty, call the police!"

"Wait Patty," Sarah pleaded putting out her hand to stop the marketing director. "Mr. Jaguar, my name, my *real* name is Sarah McCaffrey. Jonathan and I were romantically involved," she said candidly. "We have information that King O'Conner planned on splitting the proceeds of the books with Jonathan's research assistant. We're certain financial gain was the motive for someone cutting Jonathan's parachute cords," she concluded.

"King O'Conner is making plans to split the proceeds of the books?" Dean Jaguar mused. "I think you've been misinformed. He may have been Jonathan's manager, but the proceeds of the first book were to go to the New Mexico School of Paranormal Studies," he clarified. "It's possible the book rights may have been transferred to a named beneficiary in Jonathan's will but the contract we had with him was that one hundred percent of his portion of the proceeds funded a trust in his name for parapsychology research scholarship."

"Why was King arguing with Jonathan's research assistant about splitting the proceeds?" Sarah deliberated.

"King knew the particulars of our contract with Jonathan,

but his research assistant was not privy to our negotiations," Dean revealed. "I've known King for many years and I'm familiar with his business tactics," the executive laughed insincerely. "I'm assuming he was stringing the unwitting young man along for some kind of favor."

"I see, so King O'Conner will not personally benefit from the book sales unless he was named Jonathan's beneficiary in his will. If Jonathan didn't have children or family, it's possible King would've been designated as his heir. What about the screenplay and movie rights?" Cassandra interjected. "Were those outlined in your contract as well?"

"Jonathan was very specific about everything going directly the school," Dean Jaguar illuminated us. "I heard scuttlebutt about a possible movie deal. Believe me, I will be thrilled if that happens.

"What a wonderful gift," Sarah said as her eyes misted. "He was a good man."

"Yes he was and he'll be missed," Dean Jaguar said somberly. "It sounds as if you and Jonathan were close."

"Yes, yes we were close," Sarah divulged. "I'm determined to do everything in my power to see his killer is brought to justice. I'm sorry we lied to you."

"If I can be of assistance, please let me know," Dean Jaguar offered. "And I'm sorry we won't be doing a book deal with Jessica Hamby," he smiled. "You've given me some food for thought today and the idea is genius. I'll be reaching out to Deborah Ann Woll's agent. "

"Thank you Mr. Jaguar," I said and shook his hand. "We appreciate your time."

"What should we do now? Lucy asked as we turned

and walked away.

"Your sunglasses," Olivia said handing them back to Imogene. "We learned a lot!"

"Call Detective Kane," Imogene urged. "Here, use my phone," she offered and handed the sparkly cell phone to Sarah. "He needs to know what King O'Conner has planned."

"And Sloan Kirk may have known in advance of King's plans if they were romantically involved," Lucy speculated. "That's why she said Sarah ruined everything."

"Sarah make the call!" Imogene urged.

"Detective Kane please," Sarah asked as a gruff male voice answered on the second ring. "It's Sarah McCaffrey and I have some information regarding Jonathan Kirk's missing manuscript," she paused for what seemed an eternity. "What? I don't believe it!"

"What? What is it?" Lucy asked as we waited impatiently for her to tell us.

"Are you sure? When did this happen?" she asked mysteriously as she looked around in shock. "Yes, yes, thank you," she said and hung up.

"What? You're torturing me!" Olivia said. "What did he say?"

"This afternoon a man turned himself in claiming to be Jonathan's killer," Sarah announced. "He had the manuscript with him. They've got their man."

# CHAPTER TWELVE

"*He* showed up at the police station and confessed," Matt Lincoln told us as we waited to go for a gondola ride at the Venetian Hotel. "He's a crazed fan. King O'Conner verified that he'd been coming to Comic Con for years for the 'meet and greet' with the authors. He always thought the guy was a bit weird, but never imagined he'd do something as deadly as cut the parachute cords."

"Did he say why he did it?" Sarah asked as she involuntarily shivered. She pulled her red bolero style jacket tighter against her and crossed her arms. She tucked her chin and looked down at the ground.

"He admitted the whole thing. He said he was forcing Jonathan to acknowledge his research as legitimate and relevant to the field of parapsychology. The guy is a full-blown stalker. Detective Kane said he provided details of trailing the professor from Comic Con to his hotel. They have video of him in the hallway waiting for Jonathan to leave his room and again following him in the parking garage," Matt surmised.

"You mentioned research. Was he one of Jonathan's students?" Lucy inquired.

"The New Mexico police are looking into it. Right now, there not certain if he was a graduate student or independent researcher," Lincoln shared.

"How did he know we were going skydiving?" Sarah asked thoughtfully as if a fog were lifting from her brain.

"He claims he followed you in his rental car. He had a detailed log of the professor's movements and took pictures with his phone. He was obsessive."

"It certainly sounds like it," Imogene agreed. "Did the professor mention anything to you about this man, what was his name again?"

"Anthony West," Cassandra read out loud as she checked the news feed on her cell phone. "He's plastered all over the Internet. He looks relatively harmless."

"How did he get the manuscript?" Sarah asked quietly. "I'm still trying to put the pieces together."

"He said he slipped into the locker room after he cut the parachute cords and went through the professor's bag. He took the manuscript along with a watch."

"Why take a watch? Was it valuable and he going to try to pawn it?" Olivia wondered.

"The watch was a trophy item," Lincoln explained. "It's common in crimes like this for the killer to take a memento of the deceased."

"How could he possibly know which pack belonged to Jonathan?" Cassandra asked disconcerted. "And how was he able to move about the skydiving center without being spotted by someone. I don't remember seeing him, do you?"

she asked the group of us while she passed her phone around for us to view his picture.

"I didn't see him, but I was in the ladies locker room part of the time," Imogene reported.

"Olivia and I arrived after everyone was dressed. I don't remember seeing anyone other than the skydiving center personnel," I said wracking my brain. Anthony West looked like your average next door neighbor. He was dressed in a checked shirt, a navy windbreaker and thick glasses. His slightly puffy face and sagging jowls suggested to me he was in his late forties. His mug shot didn't offer any clues as to what motivated him to kill.

"I don't recall seeing him around the skydiving center," Lucy said defeated. "I wish I had. It could've made all the difference in the world."

"We can't blame ourselves for what happened," Shane spoke up. "This was the act of a very disturbed man. He'd obviously followed Jonathan for a long time. I'm thankful no one else was injured as part of the collateral damage."

"You're right," I agreed and kissed him on the cheek. "What if someone else used that pack?"

"That wouldn't have happened," Sarah shook her head. "Jonathan was the only one who jumped solo. The other packs were for tandem jumping. It was deliberate. I'm still confused as to why he took Jonathan's manuscript."

"He claims Jonathan stole his research," Lincoln informed her. "His version is his thesis was rejected by the professor and the next thing he knew, it had been published. He said it was an act of revenge for what was rightfully his in the first place."

"I'm not sure what to think right now," Sarah confessed. "I'm learning things about Jonathan I'd never have suspected. Maybe he did steal this man's research ideas."

"Stop talking nonsense," Imogene counseled. "He's not here to defend himself. You're going to take the word of a delusional homicidal maniac and let him change your opinion of Jonathan?"

"I believed everything he told me," Sarah cried. "But after what I've heard today, I don't know what to think anymore. Between Sloan Kirk, King O'Conner, Jonathan's research assistant and now this fruit loop, who knows the truth of what happened?" she concluded as she stepped out of the line and ran towards the ladies room.

"Leave her alone and give her space to regain her composure," Lucy advised. "She's overwhelmed and she needs a good cry. She'll join us when she's ready."

"I don't think she needs to be alone right now," I argued. "All this new information about Jonathan has done a head trip on her."

"It's our turn next," Olivia announced. "We should get Sarah."

"She knows we have reservations at Carnevino in an hour. She'll find us," Cassandra counseled.

"Do you think Mario Batali will be cooking tonight?" Olivia asked excitedly.

"You never know," Cassandra laughed as a dark haired gondolier took her hand and assisted her into the gondola. "Don't tell me you're a closet Mario Batali fan?"

"Paula Deen is my favorite *Food Network Star*, but there's something about a man who wears orange Crocs,"

Olivia sheepishly grinned.

"Lincoln, you'd better invest in a pair of those clogs," Shane advised.

"Not happening," Lincoln smiled and assisted Olivia into the wobbly vessel.

"We'll get the next one," Lucy volunteered as we filled the seats on the boat. "I'm sure Sarah will make the next gondola."

"We'll meet you at the palazzo landing," I called out as our gondola ride drifted through Las Vegas's rendition of the Grand Canal. The view of the shops, the bustling crowds, and the live accordion music had me reminiscing about my visit to Venice's St. Mark's square. I leaned back against Shane's chest and deeply exhaled.

"What's wrong?" he whispered in my ear. "You need to relax. The police have him in custody. Try to enjoy the rest of the trip."

"Everything seems to be up in the air," I quietly told him. "Sarah's heartbroken over Jonathan and Cassandra is returning home to face an FBI investigation. I'm worried about both of them."

"They know we're here for them," Shane said calmly. "Eventually life will get back to normal."

"It doesn't seem like it. Things have irrevocably changed with Doug. Cassandra's moving ahead with her life and Sarah has managed once again to get tangled up with someone who didn't deserve her."

"Sarah will have to realize that for herself. Regarding Cassandra she may end up being happier in the long run. Time heals all wounds," Shane offered encouragingly. "Look at Olivia and Matt. They're happy."

The two were cuddled together in their seats soaking up the atmosphere as our gondola glided through the water. Matt was whispering in Olivia's ear and bestowing kisses on her face. Her face radiated happiness.

"They do make a wonderful couple," I agreed.

"And you thought no one would ever keep up with Olivia. Sarah's time will come and I predict Cassandra will find inner peace again. I dare say more was going on at the Reynolds household than we'll ever know. She may be relived all this is coming to an end."

I looked over at Cassandra who was smiling as we floated along the canal. She seemed more relaxed than she had been at the start of our week. Maybe Doug's departure had been beneficial. Bunking with the girls had kept her mind focused on things other than the upcoming media frenzy that would greet her on our return to Dogwood Cove.

"Here we are," Shane said as we slid to a smooth stop at the palazzo landing. I was dumbfounded when I spotted the fresco on the ceiling depicting the sky and clouds. The painting actually made the enormous palazzo look as though it were high noon instead of seven PM. The architectural elements of the buildings and second floor balconies resembled places I had seen in Italy.

"This is lovely," I sighed as we exited the gondola. "Look at the acrobats performing over there. They're spinning plates! It's just like a trip to Rome," I exclaimed delighted.

"Do you hear that woman singing opera?" Cassandra joined us as we began turning around marveling at the sights. "She's fabulous!"

"Imogene and Lucy's gondola just docked," Olivia informed us as she turned towards the landing. Matt assisted each of them as they disembarked from the wobbly vessel.

"Marco, it was a pleasure meeting you," Aunt Imogene cooed as she cast a wicked glance at the muscular gondolier. "I hope we meet again."

"The pleasure was all mine," he said and tipped his hat. "Enjoy the rest of your stay in Las Vegas."

"Do you have a business card?" Imogene requested hopefully.

"Stop flirting and join the group," Lucy admonished her. "You're making a spectacle of yourself."

"I'm having fun, something you should try to do every once in a great while," she countered. "Thank you Marco!"

"Ciao Bella!" he called out as he pushed away from the landing.

"I love the Italians," Imogene declared.

"And the French, and the Spanish and the…" Lucy trailed off.

"You two ladies are a hoot!" Cassandra joined in the fun. "Where's Sarah? Didn't she make it in time for the gondola?"

"She's probably at the restaurant. I'm sure a walk gave her time to collect her thoughts," Lucy proposed.

"We should head over there in case she's waiting," I advised Shane.

"Look, gelato!" Olivia called out as we approached Cocolini's Gelatos. "What flavor does everyone want?"

"Maybe after dinner," I recommended. "I'm not filling up before I enjoy Mario's Italian cuisine."

"I'll have a single scoop of pistachio," Olivia told the

friendly lady behind the counter. "What? It's one scoop and I'm starving. I'll just skip the bread before dinner."

"I didn't say a thing this time," Cassandra joked. "Why not have dessert before dinner?"

"That's precisely my point! We're here to have fun!" Olivia declared and licked her light green gelato. "Oh 'Mama Mia!' This is delicious!"

As we made our way over to Carnevino I scanned the sea of tourists for a glimpse of Sarah's red bolero jacket. I knew she'd enjoy the street performers and I kept scanning the crowd in hopes of finding her. Tonight would be a good distraction for her. The police had Jonathan's killer and she could rest knowing he was behind bars. Case closed.

"I don't see her anywhere," I shouted over the din of people. "Do you think she went back to the hotel?"

"It's a possibility," Shane agreed. "Call her."

We reached the hostess stand outside of Carnevino and Sarah wasn't there. Shane was right. A phone call could clear all this up. On the fourth ring, I heard Sarah's muffled voice as she called out, "Amelia is that you?"

"It's me. Where are you? We're at the restaurant."

"Get off the phone. Hang it up now!" a man's angry voice was overheard in the background.

"Sarah? Where are you?" I cried as panic rose in my throat. I felt as though I would be sick.

"Amelia, I'm …" and then we were disconnected.

"Matt, call Detective Kane. Sarah's in trouble!"

# CHAPTER THIRTEEN

"Were you able to trace her cell phone signal?" I grabbed Detective Kane's arm as we reached his desk. "Please tell me you know where she is."

"She wasn't on the phone long enough to trace the signal. I'm proceeding on the assumption she was inside the Venetian Hotel when the call was made. My men are headed over there now. We'll find her," he vowed. "Did you recognize the male voice in the background?"

"No, I didn't but I can tell you he was angry," I reasoned.

"Where specifically did you last see Miss McCaffrey?" he got out his notebook.

"We last saw her at the entrance to the gondola ride," I told him. "She was upset and decided to go off by herself. We assumed she'd meet us later for our dinner reservations."

"Why do you think she's in trouble?" he queried. "Was she having a problem with someone?"

"I'm concerned her disappearance may have had something to do with a discussion we overheard earlier today," Olivia offered, "a rather heated argument between King

O'Conner and Jonathan Kirk's ghost writer."

"When did this happen?" the detective queried. There was a long uncomfortable silence as we looked at each other not certain if we should confess our afternoon exploits.

"I can't help your friend if I don't know what's going on," the officer reminded us.

"I'd like to know what's going on," Matt Lincoln said leaning over to peer down into his wife's face. "Why would Sarah go near King O'Conner?"

"She wasn't alone. We were all with her," Imogene confessed. "We took a trip to Comic Con."

"Remind me not to tell any family secrets to you," Lucy fussed. "You're like that tell-all dog Jake in the Bush's Beans commercials."

"If we want to help Sarah, Detective Kane needs to know everything," Imogene stated.

"Start at the beginning. What were you ladies doing at Comic Con?" he spoke decisively.

"After our run in with Sloan Kirk and King O'Conner, something wasn't adding up," Cassandra told him taking a seat. "We didn't want to see Sarah accused of stealing Jonathan Kirk's manuscript, so we decided to do our own background check on King O'Conner."

"You didn't, Cassandra!" Matt Lincoln barked. "I told you to stay out of it and let the police investigate."

"We have the manuscript. Your friend is off the hook," Keith Kane reported. "I don't understand what King O'Conner has to do with any of this."

"At the time we didn't know you had a suspect in custody and the manuscript had been found," I reminded him.

"King was arguing with Jonathan's ghost writer about splitting everything fifty-fifty when the second book, *Bridging the Transition*, is published," Imogene sang like a canary.

*"Bridging the Transition?* The transition to what?" the officer looked puzzled.

"That's the name of the next book, *Bridging the Transition*. King O'Conner was arguing with a young man who was the research assistant on Jonathan's last two books. He was angry he wasn't receiving credit for his work.

"Anthony West had the manuscript with him and the title of the book was *A Ghost's View of the After Life.*"

"King O'Conner and a young man were arguing about Jonathan's next book. It definitely had a different title," Cassandra ascertained.

"How can you be sure they were speaking about Jonathan Kirk?" the bewildered officer asked. "Maybe the ghost writer was another of King's clients?"

"Because he threatened to go to *Skeptic Magazine* and tell everyone he had researched and written both books and Jonathan Kirk was a phony," Imogene pronounced.

"Sounds like your guy in lockup could be a fame seeker," Matt Lincoln speculated. "Not one of us remembers seeing him at the skydiving center. Were his prints on the pack or the cut cord?"

"No, that's had me puzzled all day. But he had the missing manuscript or up until now what I assumed was the missing manuscript."

"And then there's the surveillance video. He was definitely following the professor," Lincoln agreed. "Maybe he's like that creep who was obsessed with JonBenet Ramsey."

"I'm not following you," Shane said.

"The guy who falsely confessed to murdering JonBenet Ramsey," Lincoln patiently explained. "He definitely was a sick guy, but he falsely confessed for the attention from the media."

"Rick, we need to put out an APB for Sarah McCaffrey and King O'Conner," Detective Kane yelled out across the station. "We'll get down to the bottom of this." He jumped up and strode out of the room.

"Where's he going?" Olivia asked surprised.

"My guess is he's going to interrogate Anthony West again," Lincoln speculated. "He knows he has the wrong guy behind bars. He's confronting him with the cracks in his story."

"What do we do in the meantime?" I cried. "We can't just sit here and wait. We've got to find Sarah."

"First I want to hear the whole story from the beginning," Lincoln demanded. "And don't leave out any details."

"All the details? Can't we just hit the high points?" Olivia attempted to negotiate.

"All the details Liv. If we're going to find Sarah, I need to know exactly what you know," he reasoned.

"Fine. From the beginning. We went to Leo's House of Haunts for costumes to wear at Comic Con," Olivia recited.

"Please tell me you didn't," Lincoln whined wiping his hands down his face in utter exasperation. "What did I tell you about keeping your nose clean?"

"Stop worrying. He didn't even recognize us," Imogene said proudly. "The Klingon costumes were perfect."

"Klingons? Oh, I've got to hear this," Shane chuckled. "Go ahead Liv, I'm listening."

"A unit picked up O'Conner and they're headed to the station," Keith Kane announced as he strode back over to his desk.

"Sarah wasn't with him?" I asked deflated.

"No, she wasn't. I need more details about this man you saw arguing with King O'Conner. If I can get a sketch artist in here, do you think you could give an accurate description?"

"Yes I can, absolutely," I agreed. "I think we all can help with that."

"The faster we get this done, the faster we will find your friend," Kane said with determination.

❧    ❧    ❧

"His eyes were closer together," I recalled trying my best to describe his face. "His hair was tousled and he had a scruffy five o'clock shadow."

"It was more than a five o'clock shadow," Olivia corrected me. "It was a short beard and not very well-kept I might add."

"Did he have any distinguishing marks on his face? A mole, a scar?" the sketch artist asked as he quickly added details to the paper.

"No, but he did have a gap between his front teeth. He could benefit from some orthodontia," Lucy remarked.

"The things you notice," Shane laughed as we continued to watch the officer at work. Little by little a face was emerging that eerily resembled the ghost writer.

"Was he wearing anything that could help identify him? An earring, a necklace, a hoodie?" the officer prompted our collective memories.

"I don't remember anything like jewelry, do you?" I asked the group.

"He had on a turquoise and silver watch," Imogene noted.

"I didn't see a watch," Lucy remarked.

"This watch was unique," Imogene explained. "It had an antique look to it as if it were a relic."

"And when did you become the upmost authority on antique jewelry?" Lucy needled her.

"I watch *Antique Roadshow* on PBS. I've picked up a couple of pointers. You never would guess some of the art and objects found in attics could be so valuable."

"Back to our suspect," Cassandra directed our attention. "Anyone else remember anything remarkable about him?"

"He was wearing jeans and a plaid short sleeved shirt, the kind all the young people wear these days," Lucy added.

"You need to make the cheek bones slightly more prominent," Olivia advised the officer as she leaned over his shoulder. "I think that's looks just like him. What do you think?"

"I agree. Detective Kane can show this sketch to King O'Conner and ask him who this man is and how he's involved with Sarah's disappearance," I said firmly.

"I'll put a BOLO out with this picture," the sketch artist told us as he quickly left the conference room and headed down the hall.

"Let's hope he gets a lead with that sketch," I said as I took Shane's hand for support.

"He will. Here's the detective now," Shane said as he stood as Keith Kane addressed our group.

"We've got your guy," he said waving the paper around.

"Thank goodness! That was fast!" Cassandra sighed and looked around at us optimistically. "Where did you find him?"

"We found him at the Bellagio about an hour ago," Detective Kane announced. "His body was found floating in the fountain. He had a fatal gunshot to the head."

# CHAPTER FOURTEEN

"*I* can't sit around here waiting for the police to find her. We need to go out and look for Sarah," Olivia said with determination.

"No one is going anywhere until Matt gets back from the station," Shane commanded. "I'm not having anyone else get hurt or disappear under my watch," he said firmly and crossed his arms defiantly. "The wise thing to do is let the police do their job."

"A fine job they're doing," Olivia rebutted. "First Jonathan is murdered and now this Skylar Lawrence guy."

"The two murders could be unrelated," I pointed out. "Let's not jump to conclusions."

"Amelia, you were there. You heard the argument between that kid, Skylar, and King O'Conner. He threatened to send a DVD to *Skeptic Magazine* if anything happened to him," Olivia debated with me. "And now the guy is dead!"

"The police are investigating the homicide," Shane informed us. "The best thing for us to do is wait to see how the questioning with King O'Conner goes and see if they develop any new leads."

"I'm worried this time Sarah's in over her head. This isn't the first time she's gone off with some harebrained scheme to catch a killer. What's taking Lincoln so long?" I asked irritably. The long day had left us weary and my patience had worn thin.

"Interrogations take time. It's like a well-practiced dance. You let the suspect think you know something and he gradually confesses little by little. If King O'Conner knows where Sarah is he's probably spilling his guts right now. Two people are dead associated with that manuscript and he's the common thread," Olivia ventured.

"I'd like to wrap this up and top it with a bow too, but something's not adding up and I can't put my finger on it," Cassandra ruminated.

"It's like the professor said," Imogene submitted, "it's that little voice that's speaking to you. There's more to this than meets the eye."

"You can cut the detective act, Angela Lansbury!" Lucy cackled.

The door lock turned and Matt Lincoln joined us in the living room. We were relieved to see him and hopeful he had information as to Sarah's whereabouts.

"What did the bastard say?" Olivia demanded to know clinching her fists. "What's he done with Sarah?"

"He swears he has nothing to do with Sarah's disappearance. He was taken aback when Kane confronted him with what you ladies overheard at Comic Con. It looks like he's the primary suspect in the shooting of Skylar Lawrence," he informed us. "The police have confirmed King O'Conner was named Jonathan's beneficiary in his will. Without your information, the police wouldn't have known the motive for Jonathan or Skylar's murders."

"Did he admit it?" Lucy asked dumbfounded.

"He's not saying anything. He's asked for his attorney," Matt said dejectedly. "They're not any closer to finding Sarah," Matt said dejectedly.

"I think the best course of action we can take is to wait to hear from the police," Olivia stated executing a complete one hundred eighty. "She may try to contact us. We should stay close to our phones and wait to hear from her."

"That's not what you said a minute ago," I muttered under my breath.

"I've changed my mind, Amelia. I want to be a help, not a hindrance," Olivia quietly told me. "You guys have been so frantic worrying about Sarah, why don't you go out and grab a beer, play a few hands of black jack and we'll keep posted here. I'll call your cell phone the moment I hear anything."

"There's no way I'm letting up on the investigation," Lincoln avowed. "I'm heading back to the station to see if there are any new leads."

"Why don't you take Shane with you and we girls can order room service. I'm so pooped, I feel as though I could fall asleep any moment," Olivia offered. She stretched her arms above her head and yawned. She did look tired.

"My poor baby is exhausted," Lincoln soothed and kissed his bride. "Why don't you ladies change into something comfortable and try to relax. We've got everything handled, don't we Shane. We can keep you updated with the case from the station."

"I'd like see you have a crack at King O'Conner," Shane agreed. "I think it's beem helpful having you at the station. I'll call and keep you updated," he promised me.

"That's fine. Please call the moment you hear anything," I requested and followed the guys to the door. I double bolted the lock and turned back towards the ladies. I looked out the peep hole and waited a few moments to make sure the men were on the elevators before speaking.

"That is some of the worst acting I've ever seen, Olivia Rivers Lincoln." I smiled and shook my index finger at her. "You're up to no good."

"There's one person who may know where Sarah is," Olivia thought aloud. "Skylar Lawrence said if anything happened to him, he was sending a DVD to Brian Myers. We find Brian Myers we find the missing piece to this puzzle."

"So you're proposing we go and speak with Brian Myers," Lucy said impressed. "What if your husband calls looking for you?"

"I'm asleep. I didn't hear the phone ring," Olivia adlibbed. "Besides they'll be gone for hours playing *Starsky and Hutch.*"

"I could stay here by the phone and if Shane or Matt calls, you're both asleep," Imogene offered. "Shane would never suspect me of fibbing to him. It would buy more time."

"And that gives you time to locate Brian Myers. How do you plan to find him?" Lucy asked doubtfully.

"We start here, *Skeptic's Magazine,*" Cassandra replied tossing a periodical in her direction. "I have a few journalism contacts that may tell me where to find Brian Myers. I'll make a few calls and see what I can unearth!"

She returned to the living room of the suite ten minutes later looking elated.

"You'll never guess who's in Vegas for Comic Con!" she screamed. "I've got his hotel information. Let's head over there now."

"Wait, shouldn't we call him first?" I agonized. "What if he's not there?"

"I don't think we should give him a head's up," Cassandra disagreed. "If he's not there, we wait for him."

"It's late," Olivia realized. "He's probably out gambling or at a show."

"You may be right and if he is, we'll wait," Cassandra decided. She grabbed her Nikon camera bag from the table.

"And I'll wait here with Imogene," Lucy volunteered. "There's no sense in all of us going to speak with this Myers man."

"Be careful, girls," Imogene cautioned giving us each a hug. "Call me the minute you know something."

"I promise we will," I said hurrying out the door with my handbag and jacket. "Where are we going, Cassandra?"

"He's staying at the Venetian Hotel, Room six fourteen!" Cassandra said out of breath as we hustled towards the elevator.

"The Venetian? Do you think that's a coincidence?" I considered.

"I doubt it. I think Brian Myers may be more involved than we realized," she speculated.

We hailed a taxi outside of the Bellagio and were quickly delivered to the front entrance of the Venetian, right where we had stood awaiting our gondola ride a few hours earlier.

We rushed past the bellmen and found the bank of elevators. A short ride to the sixth floor deposited us in the hallway leading to room six hundred fourteen.

"Put this camera over your shoulder," Cassandra directed me and lifted her hand to knock on the door.

"Wait. Before we knock, what are we going to say?" Olivia asked organizing her thoughts. "Our friend is missing and we think you may know something? Or hand over the DVD and no one will get hurt?"

"Nice try, 'red,' but neither approach works. I have a plan," Cassandra calmed her. "Follow my lead and please do your best to keep quiet no matter what. Sarah's life may be in danger and if we handle Mr. Meyers with kid gloves, he may lead us to her."

Cassandra rapped loudly on the door. A muffled noise could be heard from within and a low conversation. A few seconds later, a middle-aged man opened the door and looked cross as he stood before us wearing nothing but a towel wrapped around his waist.

"Can I help you?" he asked with irritation evident in his voice. We had certainly interrupted a private moment between the man and whoever else was inside the suite.

"Hello, Mr. Meyers, I'm Cassandra Reynolds, a close personal friend of John M. Geddes, managing editor of *The New York Times*," she said smiling at the confused man. "He's asked me to interview you for a story we are doing on Comic Con and he advised me that a fresh perspective on the event was in order. Who better to offer a unique viewpoint than you, Mr. Meyers, editor of *Skeptic Magazine?*"

"I'm sorry, you caught me at a bad time," he said flustered.

"I wasn't aware that John Geddes was a fan of my magazine," he said looking rather pleased.

"He's a huge fan of *Skeptic Magazine,*" Cassandra continued blowing smoke up his towel. "In fact, he'd like me to take a few pictures of you for our feature article on Comic Con."

"He wants my picture and comments? Please forgive my manners, Ms. Reynolds. If you'll give me just a few minutes, I could meet you downstairs at the lounge where we can speak more freely," he indicated with his head towards the room.

"Absolutely, take your time," Cassandra beamed quite pleased with herself. "We'll meet you in the lounge and I'll have my photographer take some test shots," she said indicating my camera. I hesitated for just a moment before patting the camera case and smiling at the half-naked man.

"Thank you. This is a tremendous opportunity," he said nervously with enthusiasm. "I'll be right down," he said and shut the door.

We walked partially down the hall before speaking.

"You're a genius Cassandra. When did you come up with the whole interview idea?" I asked.

"People in the news business love being a part of the news. It's a win-win for him if his magazine is featured in a publication as large as *The New York Times.* It gives his publication credibility. He couldn't refuse my request and my guess is whoever was in the hotel room with him is going to be sadly disappointed their visit will be cut short.

"What's next? A fake photo shoot in the lounge?" I guessed.

"We may not get to that point. I'm going to ambush him

with the information about the DVD and Skylar Lawrence's murder," she said assuredly.

"I feel bad we interrupted his date," Olivia sniggered. "It's probably not often he gets lucky."

"Olivia, you're so bad," I laughed as I smacked her arm playfully. "Maybe he's a real Don Juan."

"Not in my book. I like a man with a six-pack and I don't mean beer," she joked as we made our way down the elevator to the lobby. The doorway to the lounge was located across from the elevators. "We can wait here for him," she suggested as we found a comfortable spot on a long settee. "Do they have anything to nibble on at the bar? I'm starving! We never ate dinner."

"I'm sure they have nuts or cocktail mix," Cassandra told her. "He may be a while since he's having his picture taken. He'll probably take a few minutes to think out his wardrobe."

"Do you think he already has the DVD?" I asked as Olivia made her way over to the Italian marble bar at the opposite end of the lobby.

"Skylar Lawrence said he was leaving instructions to have it delivered if anything happened to him," Cassandra reflected. "It hasn't been that long since the police found his body. It hasn't hit the news yet," she reported looking at the newsfeed on her cell phone.

"Do you think he may have been bluffing about the DVD? What if he only said that to keep King O'Conner from cutting him out of the book deal?" I deduced.

"That's always a possibility. If I were a betting man, I would wager Skylar Lawrence made a DVD. This manuscript had a possible movie deal attached to it. That's big money and I've heard there's already a buzz about Jonathan's book. They're talking about M. Night Shyamalan directing it since he received such acclaim with the *Sixth Sense.*"

"I love that movie. It was nominated for best picture and best director," I added.

"Did you find something to munch on?" Cassandra asked as Olivia walked back to us and sat down.

"They had a nice antipasto bar, but you had to order a drink. I'm afraid if I have a cocktail, I might fall asleep," Olivia told us. "So I got a cola instead."

"I know what you mean. It's been a long night and Sarah's still missing. I wish we had a clue as to where Sarah might be," I said somberly.

"There's your clue," Olivia said loudly and rose up and pointed towards the elevator doors. Holding hands with Brian Myers was Sloan Kirk! She stopped to give him a passionate kiss before he came towards us.

"Stop her!" Olivia yelled to a nearby bellman as she abruptly set her drink down and began to run towards the unsuspecting woman. "Don't let her get away!" she screamed as she lunged at an unsuspecting Sloan Kirk and brought her down with a hard tackle to the marble floor.

"What's going on?" Brian Myers demanded as he tried to move Olivia off the thrashing woman.

"Get this crazy woman off of me!" Sloan Kirk screamed up at the astonished man.

"You're lucky we got to you in time!" Olivia informed him. "She's a 'black widow' and you might have been her next victim!" she said as she continued to pin down the emaciated female.

"What are you talking about? We just met in the casino," he said defensively.

The hotel security ran over and peeled Olivia off of the disheveled ex-wife of Jonathan Kirk. "Arrest her," Sloan demanded and pointed at Olivia. "She attacked me!"

"Call Detective Keith Kane. You need to hold her until they get here. He's going to want to bring her in for questioning," she ordered.

"She's telling the truth," Cassandra joined the frenzy. "Detective Kane has her cohort in custody at the station. He's being investigated for the death of Skylar Lawrence," she told the security team.

"Skylar Lawrence is dead?" Brian Myers asked in shock. "I just spoke with him this morning."

"You need to sit down," Cassandra urged him. "Let's go somewhere where it's a little quieter and we can talk in private."

"But what about Sheila?" he asked as he watched the security team escort Sloan Kirk to the office followed by Olivia. "I don't understand what's going on."

"Sheila? Is that what she told you her name was?" I asked. "Her name is Sloan Kirk. She's the ex-wife of Jonathan Kirk," I informed him as he continued to look dazed.

"She's involved with King O'Conner, Jonathan Kirk's manager and she plans to publish his final manuscript. I'm sorry to have to tell you this, but you were a pawn in her scheme to financially benefit from his death."

"I'm going to need a stiff drink," he admitted. "Back up and let's start at the beginning."

Cassandra patiently laid out the details of Jonathan's murder, about the exchange between Skylar and King and the disappearance of Sarah. He quickly downed his first scotch and motioned to the bartender for a second drink.

"So you're not actually with *The New York Times?*" he asked sounding rather disappointed. "You're looking for your friend."

"I'm sorry I lied to you, but you're the key in this mystery," Cassandra shared. "Skylar Lawrence was entrusting you with the truth about the manuscript if anything happened to him. He promised King O'Conner he would send you a DVD if anything happened to him and my guess is that Sloan Kirk planned to ransack your hotel room to find it."

"I did speak to Skylar this morning," the editor told us as his hand trembled when he raised his glass to his lips. He took a long sip of scotch and set the glass down. "I blame myself for what's happened to him," he said suddenly distraught.

"You couldn't know he'd be murdered," Cassandra attempted to reassure him. "How could you have prevented his death?"

"He was working for me," Brian Myers explained. "He's been undercover for my magazine for some time. Jonathan Kirk and his paranormal school of research is one of *Skeptic Magazine's* top targets. We've been trying to get the dirt on the program for years. Skylar Lawrence was hired to expose the school."

"And it's director, Jonathan Kirk," Cassandra construed. "Were you aware Skylar was ghost writing on Jonathan's books?"

"Yes, I knew. He would e-mail me copies of the manuscript and our team was putting together a full investigation of the research. Our plan was to prove Jonathan was a phony," he concluded. "The story would have sold millions of copies of our magazine."

"So you were waiting for the right time to shed light on Jonathan," Cassandra guessed. "And you didn't mind to pay Skylar to co-author the books."

"Not only did I pay Skylar, I planned on exposing Jonathan at Comic Con," the newsman confessed. "And then he died. It didn't seem the decent thing to do. I decided to hold the story and report it at a more appropriate time."

"That's not what you newsmen do," Cassandra disputed the story. "It would have made an even bigger splash to have done it now. What did they have on you? Was it Skylar or King who was blackmailing you?"

"I never said anything about blackmail," Meyers sputtered. "Why makes you think I was being blackmailed?"

"Because you're wearing a wedding ring and Sloan Kirk, aka Sheila, is not Mrs. Myers. This wasn't the first time this week you've hooked up with her, is it? It's obvious you were being double crossed by your own undercover reporter. Did he have pictures of you with Mrs. Kirk? Seems Skylar was quite the double agent," Cassandra said knowingly. "That's why you chose not to discredit Jonathan Kirk. You were covering your own derriere!"

"I've worked too hard to build up my magazine. I can't afford a personal problem right now. If my wife found out about this, I would be financially ruined!" he sighed loudly and took another sip of his scotch. "He met with me this morning to tell me he had a sex tape of Sheila, I mean Sloan, and me."

"What is it about this woman that is so alluring? Never mind, don't answer that!" I said aloud.

"The police are on their way," Olivia informed us as she took a seat. "Does he have any idea where Sarah is?"

"He doesn't know any more than we do," I sadly reported. "I think when Detective Kane gets here he'll want to question Mr. Myers.

"He has the DVD?" Olivia supposed.

"No, but he has information that will explains why Skylar Lawrence was threatening King O'Conner. Unfortunately for you Mr. Myers, you will be a suspect as well."

"Are you kidding me? Suspected for what?"

"You're a suspect in the murder of Skylar Lawrence. You admitted he was blackmailing you."

"I leave for ten minutes and I miss everything!" Olivia moaned.

"I'll get you up to speed," I told her as Detective Kane arrived. "Detective, you're going to want to question this man in the death of Skylar Lawrence."

# CHAPTER FIFTEEN

"*You* ladies are tough," Detective Kane said proudly. "Do you realize thanks to you, we have Skylar Lawrence's murderer behind bars?"

"GSR will get you every time," Olivia said knowingly.

"What's GSR dear?" Imogene asked.

"Gunshot residue," Detective Kane explained. "There were traces of gunpowder on King's hands when we tested him. We located the gun in the fountain. He shot Skylar during one of the shows so no one would hear the gunshot over the noise."

"It was the perfect crime," I observed.

"And all because of greed," Lucy said sadly.

"Yes, Skylar Lawrence realized the potential financial gain in having the book published and the subsequent movie deals. An undercover story for *Skeptic's Magazine* didn't have the same payout. Had he succeeded, he would've been a wealthy young man," the police officer commented.

"Brian Myers didn't have anything to do with it?" I guessed and the officer shook his head in the affirmative.

"He's been released," Matt Lincoln spoke up.

"Has King admitted to having a hand in Sarah's disappearance? The way I see it, Sloan and King were scheming together. She was in the way," I ventured.

"Neither of them claims to know anything about Miss McCaffrey. We're trying to locate her cell phone signal, but we think the battery has been removed. We haven't had a ping from her signal in the last several hours," he said solemnly.

"They know something," Olivia argued. "Let me have five minutes with that science experiment. I can break her!"

"And we'd have to bail you out for assault," Lincoln said shaking his head at his wife.

"Let me see if I have the facts straight," I said aloud. "Anthony West killed Jonathan Kirk for some kind of revenge for stealing a thesis he was working on, King O'Conner shot Skylar Lawrence to keep one hundred percent of the money earned from any book or movie deals, and Sloan Kirk was sleeping with everyone," I joked.

"It doesn't make sense that the manuscript Anthony West stole is different from the manuscript Skylar Lawrence was working on. I still don't understand it," Olivia commented. "I keep trying to wrap my brain around it."

"He could by lying about it," Shane reminded us. "After all, none of us saw Anthony West at the skydiving center."

"What could he possibly gain by lying? And the manuscript, whichever one was in his duffle bag, wasn't there after Jonathan's accident," I recalled.

"We have to assume since he followed Jonathan around without being detected, it's possible he was at the skydiving center and we didn't notice him," Lincoln ascertained. "There's video of him following the professor that day in the parking garage. He could have been watching from anywhere in the hangar. He waited for the opportune moment when no one was around and cut the cords to his parachutes. After we took off in the plane he let himself into the men's locker room and stole the manuscript."

"But what if it wasn't him? The manuscripts don't match," I reiterated.

"Do you think Sarah figured it out?" Lucy supposed. "Maybe she suspected who the real culprit was and decided to go after them."

"If that's the case, she should have said something to one of us," Olivia pointed out. "But, this isn't the first time she's acted alone on a hunch."

"Yes, I vividly remember how overjoyed I was to see her when I was kidnapped," Imogene recollected. "She doesn't cower from a challenge."

"We have FBI profilers talking with Anthony West right now. They'll be able to determine with a degree of certainty whether he's claiming to have murdered Mr. Kirk for fame or for revenge for a stolen thesis."

"I remember when I was watching an episode of *Criminal Minds* there was a suspect in custody who was confessing to a murder for the fame. They figured it out and they caught the real killer," Olivia told us.

"Here she goes quoting *Criminal Minds*. Olivia, what am I going to do with you?" Cassandra shrugged her shoulders.

"What? It's a great show and many of the episodes are based on actual cases!"

"Detective, we got a ping from her cell phone!" an officer interrupted as he rushed towards Keith Kane's desk. "It came from a tower near a private airstrip."

"The skydiving center!" I yelled. "Sarah must be there looking for clues."

"Or she's being held there against her will," Lincoln ventured.

"We're going to have to handle this with the utmost caution," Kane told the other officer. "I want you to call the tactical team in right away. We don't want to tip anyone's hand that we've got a location."

"Right boss!" the officer said and headed to his desk to make the call.

"If she's at the skydiving center and her cell phone is working, she would've called us by now," Lucy worried. "Something's definitely wrong."

# CHAPTER SIXTEEN

*W*e quietly arrived at the skydiving center. Dawn was breaking and the desert sky was painted in hues of pink and lavender. My spirits rose as I prayed the police had located Sarah. I hoped against hope this nightmare would soon be over.

"I don't care what Detective Kane said," Olivia exploded. "I'm not waiting at the hotel or the police station. If Sarah's here, she needs us!"

"We could be charged with police interference," Lucy warned. "We need to stay back and let them do their job."

"And if we had stayed in our room and waited for them to investigate like they asked us to do, they'd never know about Skylar Lawrence or Brian Myers. I think we've proven ourselves and earned the right to be here," Olivia opined. "She's our friend. No one can stop me from being here for Sarah."

Olivia could be acerbic with her viewpoints and was often hardest on those closest to her, but when it came down to being dependable and loyal to her friends, no one was her equal.

Detective Kane stealthily disappeared into the entrance of the skydiving center. The bay doors were closed and didn't afford us a view as to what was going on inside.

"The lights are out and I can't see a thing from here," Olivia complained. "I'm going to have to get closer."

"One step closer and I'll have to put you in the back of the squad car," Matt Lincoln halfway joked with his wife. "I don't need you getting shot or hurt. We're simply here to assist."

"You don't think I'd seriously go inside? I was kidding!" she defended herself.

"And this coming from the woman who tackled Sloan Kirk in the lobby of the Venetian Hotel? I don't believe you for a second," he snarked.

"Who told you about that?" she looked displeased.

"The head of security at the Venetian, the arresting officer, and a dozen other policemen. You've got quite a reputation with the LVPD, Mrs. Lincoln."

"I can't tell if you're proud or angry with me," Olivia said looking up into the face of her tall husband.

"We can discuss all that later. Right now, let's stay back and let Detective Kane do his job," he advised all of us.

"And I'm here to keep an eye on the rest of you ladies," Shane reminded us. "I can't believe you fooled us into thinking you were resting at the hotel."

"A girl's got to do what a girl's got to do," Olivia said smugly.

"And that may be why Sarah's in trouble," Matt reminded her. "She didn't wait for the police, but thought she would investigate by herself. Let's hope she's Ok."

"I have all the faith in the world she is," I told him. "She managed to get her cell phone turned back on as a signal. She knew we'd find her.

Detective Kane returned from the doorway and motioned for the SWAT team captain.

"I didn't see anyone inside. Something's fishy," we overheard him saying.

Just then I head the unmistakable roar of an airplane motor turning over.

"The plane hangar!" I shouted. "He's going to take off in the plane!"

The SWAT team descended on the building and surrounded the hangar. Much to our dismay, it was empty! The small Super King Air plane could be seen taxiing on the runway strip.

"They're going to take off!" I yelled as we all began running towards the airstrip.

"Stand back, Amelia!" Matt Lincoln ordered as he grabbed my arm to stop me. Everyone stop! You'll get hurt if you're not careful!"

"Sarah, Sarah!" I screamed over the deafening motor.

A hail of bullets bounced off the metal siding of the plane as it continued to taxi. A loud explosion echoed through the desert as a sniper expertly shot out the tires and slowed the plane. It allowed time for the SWAT team Hummer to pull in front of the plane with their guns drawn. The team's intention was to shoot the pilot through the window.

"I can't look," Olivia cried as she turned her head away. "Please tell me it's over!"

The propellers of the plane were still turning and the airplane surged forward again to be met by a hail of bullets. The plane continued to limp down the runway.

"They're going to crash!" Imogene screamed as we watched in terror. The airplane hit the barrier at the end of the landing strip and a plume of smoke shot into the sky.

"No!" Cassandra screeched and covered her eyes. We all stood frozen not sure what to do. The fire quickly spread and burned brightly.

"Wait, look!" Imogene cried as saw the side door to the airplane open and Sarah jumped out.

We immediately ran towards the airstrip to help her away from the burning plane.

"Get back!" the SWAT captain ordered as a large explosion shook the ground. The entire plane was now engulfed in flames. The heat from the fuel made the air hard to breathe. Sirens could be heard from a fire engine on its way to the scene.

"Sarah, thank God you are OK!" I cried and hugged my comrade close. "We've been frantically searching for you."

"What in the world happened to you?" Olivia halfway chastised her longtime friend. "You scared us to death!"

"I walked through the palazzo at the Venetian and it hit me. Anthony West's story wasn't adding up."

"Yeah, he had a different manuscript," Imogene agreed. "How did you figure it out?"

"It was the watch he claimed he took from Jonathan's duffle bag. Jonathan had left his pocket watch in the car before the jump. He explained to me his grandfather had given it to him and how sentimental it was to him.

I remembered the watch was in his car at the skydiving center and I came back to look for it," she communicated to us.

"And what happened?" Lucy prodded her.

"I found the pocket watch and stopped by the office to say hello and talk with Paul," Sarah recounted. "That's when he snapped and told me everything would have been OK if I hadn't stuck my nose in his business. It was then I knew I was in trouble."

"Paul? Paul was the one who sabotaged the jump?" Shane asked incredulously. "He was my tandem partner."

"And a murderer," Cassandra alleged.

"He was indebted to Jonathan for a tremendous amount of money," Sarah explained. "Paul told me he had a gambling habit and mortgaged the skydiving center to cover his debts. Jonathan loaned him money to help him out."

"And Paul continued to gamble," Lincoln speculated. "And when Jonathan approached him about the loan, he had his back against the wall."

"I'm confused," Lucy expressed. "How would it benefit him to have the professor out of the way? Was this about repaying a loan?"

"Jonathan had papers drawn up offering the skydiving center as collateral. Jonathan was trying to keep Paul from having to file bankruptcy."

"Sounds like a good friend," Shane ruminated. "I don't understand why Paul would kill him."

"Jonathan took over ownership of the center when Paul continued to gamble and didn't reimburse him. He kept Paul on as a business partner so he could continue working,"

Sarah explained. "They took life insurance policies on each other to ensure that the business survives the partner's death and provides funds to the beneficiaries of the partner. Paul planned on killing Jonathan and collecting the life insurance money. He was waiting to make his claim after the police investigation was complete."

"What a tragedy and all for greed," Imogene said dabbing her eyes with a tissue. "I'm so relieved you're safe now. You must have gone through hell!"

"He didn't hurt me," Sarah reported. "He kept me at gunpoint and I waited until he fell asleep to locate my cell phone, find the battery and put it back in. He caught me and said he was going to take me up in the plane and drop me in the middle of the desert where no one would discover me. He planned on letting me die of starvation, thirst or the injuries sustained from the drop. I kept thinking about Jonathan and how horrible it must have been for him when he was free falling and I knew if I listened to that inner voice, I'd somehow survive."

"Sarah, I can't believe this! And the police never suspected Paul!" I said incredulously.

"None of us did. Who would have thought there were issues between them? Paul seemed like such a fun-loving guy," Shane said stunned.

"And there were no fingerprints on the cord. He was careful," Olivia remembered. "Paul had been standing around with everyone before the flight. He had to pick just the right time to sever the cords."

"He had ample opportunity," Sarah pointed out. "He helped perform the safety checks on the packs."

"And when Anthony West turned himself in, case closed," Lucy inferred.

"So it seemed until that sixth sense kicked up, right honey?" Imogene asked Sarah smoothing her brown hair. "The professor was guiding you."

"I feel like he was," she broke down crying. "I think I need a long bath and some hot tea."

"Let's get you home, Sarah!" I said turning away from the airstrip.

# CHAPTER SEVENTEEN

"The trip wasn't a total bust," Shane said trying to be optimistic. "We did place third in the iced tea championships with our blackberry bramble blend and we have new orders to fill as soon as we return home."

"I know. I was expecting a bit more from this trip," I sighed and looked dejectedly from our balcony to the fountain below.

"You thought it might be more on the wild side?" he teased.

"I got more than I bargained for with this whole debacle surrounding the professor. If I wanted to experience the 'wild side' of Vegas, I would've gone out with Aunt Imogene and Lucy last night to *Thunder From Down Under*.

"I'm relieved they managed to go so I don't have to hear about it anymore," Shane laughed. "I think that's the primary reason Imogene came on this trip."

"Speaking of returning home, I know Cassandra has to be dreading it. She's going to have to face Doug and a full-blown FBI investigation.

Cassandra knocked lightly at our door and let herself in. "You don't need to worry about me, Amelia. This trip has helped put unresolved issues in perspective. We nearly lost Sarah and that made me realize life is fleeting. You've got to grab onto happiness when you have a chance. That's why I'm going to make some difficult decisions when I get home."

"Like what?" I asked as my heart filled with apprehension. "What have you decided to do about Doug?

"For starters, Doug and I are going to sit down and have a long talk. A real heart-to-heart talk with no interruptions, no cell phones, and no campaign advisors. And then we're going to decide our future and the future of Reynolds's Candies. He may not be pleased with the outcome of that discussion.

"Cassandra, don't tell me you've made up your mind about the business?" I asked sadly. "Are you going to stay on at Reynolds's as CEO?"

"I've called Rick Green and set up another meeting. This time at the headquarters of Aztec Chocolates," Cassandra shared with us. "I thought I'd better have an idea of what Aztec has to offer me, so a company tour is in order."

"Cassandra, you can't be thinking of leaving Reynolds?" Shane asked flabbergasted. "You've built that company back up when it was practically extinct!"

"And it's a good time to move on. All this nonsense with Doug and Dixie has forced me to realize we don't share the same values. I gave up having a family to be a career woman and I gave up following my own passion to run Doug's family business. I've given up plenty for him. It's time for me now," she said sternly.

"I back you one hundred percent, Cassandra. Rick Green would be lucky to have you running Aztec's especially with the nationwide expansion into the malls with his chocolate drinking bar concept. You'll be doing a lot of traveling if you take this job," I said.

"Yeah, traveling from Dogwood Cove all over the US," Shane agreed.

"No, Shane. If I take the job, I'll be moving," she reminded him. "Rick has offered me a sweet deal and I'd be a fool to pass it up. The company is located in San Francisco, so I'd be spending most of my time there."

"I guess I didn't realize you were seriously considering his offer. I'd hate to see you leave. Have you told anyone else?" Shane inquired.

"Not yet and I want to wait," Cassandra explained delicately. "Olivia and Matt are still in the honeymoon phase and she deserves to be happy right now. I don't know what it would do to her if she thought I was moving. She's already upset about my problems with Doug. I've tried so hard to be private about it and I know it's taken a toll on all of you."

"Friends are always there for each other through the thick and the thin. You know you're going to have to tell her sometime. It's best she hears it from you instead of Sally Stokes or some news reporter," I advised.

"I'm going to be spending some time at my Sonoma Valley home next month. It will give me some time to clear my head and put me closer to Aztec Chocolates. If I need to meet with Rick, I'll be a short drive or helicopter ride away."

"You've really thought about this, haven't you?" I asked

sadly. "Cassandra, it wouldn't be the same without you around."

"It's not definite. But if I decide to take the position, it's not as if we wouldn't see each other," she said with forced cheerfulness. "I'll fly to Dogwood Cove for visits and I'll have all of you out to California. I'd make sure we see each other often. Besides, it's not official yet. A lot can happen. Who knows? Maybe Doug will turn over a new leaf and sweep me off my feet again."

"Doug is a complete idiot!" Shane barked. "I can't believe how foolish he's behaved. I've lost respect for him. And now Reynolds's Candies may be losing a top-notch CEO."

"I thank you Shane for your support, but don't be angry with Doug. He's going to need his friends around him when this becomes fodder for the press. He needs someone to stand by him. Please don't turn your back on him," she urged. "But let's not let this ruin the rest of our trip. If you don't mind keeping this between us, I'd appreciate it."

"I won't say anything, but you have to tell Olivia and Sarah soon," I requested. "I can't carry around this secret."

"I will after my meeting with Rick. When I know for sure, I'll tell them. There's no sense in burdening them with that now."

"Knock, knock!" Imogene called as she poked her head into the room. "What's the powwow about?"

"Come in, come in! We were just saying how glad we are to be going home," I smiled and invited my aunt, Sarah and Lucy inside.

"I hope you don't mind, but I brought a bottle of champagne to toast the good fortune that our sweet Sarah was returned to us unharmed," Imogene sang out as she popped the cork on the bottle of bubbly. "Shoot, it spilled!" she squealed as the champagne froth went all over the floor.

"Wait for me!" Olivia yelled as she and Lincoln joined us. "I want some!"

"Here, pass the glasses around," I instructed as I handed out flutes. "Let's toast Sarah!" I said raising my glass.

"To 'The Traveling Tea Ladies!'" Sarah cheered.

"And to Sarah," we said clinking our glasses together. My eyes misted over as I looked around the group of smiling faces and realized this might be the last trip we shared together.

## ❧ THE END ☙

# How to Make
# the Perfect Pot of Tea

In the same amount of time that you measure level scoops of coffee for the coffee maker and add ounces of water, you can prepare a cup or pot of tea.

### *Step 1: Select your tea pot.*

Porcelain or pottery is the better choice versus silver plated tea pots which can impart a slightly metallic taste. Make sure your tea pot is clean with no soapy residue and prime your tea pot by filling it with hot water, letting it sit for a few minutes and then pouring the water out so that your pot will stay warm longer!

### *Step 2: WATER, WATER, WATER!*

Begin with the cleanest, filtered, de-chlorinated water you can. Good water makes a huge difference. Many of my tea room guests have asked why their tea doesn't taste the same at home. The chlorine in the water is often the culprit of sabotaging a great pot of tea.

Be sure your water comes to a rolling boil and quickly remove it. If you let it boil continuously, you will boil out all the oxygen and be left with a "flat" tasting tea. Please do not microwave your water. It can cause your water to "super boil" and lead to third degree burns. If you are in a situation where you don't have a full kitchen, purchase an electric tea kettle to quickly and easily make your hot water.

And NEVER, NEVER, EVER MAKE TEA IN A COFFEE MAKER! I cannot tell you how I cringe when asked if it's okay. Coffee drinkers don't want to taste tea and tea drinkers don't want to taste coffee. Period! End of story! Golden rule—no coffee makers!

Now that we've cleared that up, let's measure out our tea!

## Step 3: Measure Out Your Tea.

It's easy! The formula is one teaspoon of loose tea per 8 ounces of water. For example, if you are using a 4 cup teapot, you would use 4 teaspoons of tea, maybe a little less depending on your personal taste. Measure your tea and place inside a "t-sac" or paper filter made for tea, infuser ball, or tea filter basket. Place the tea inside your pot and now you're ready for steeping.

## Step 4: Steeping Times and Temperature.

*This is the key!*

> **Black teas**—Steep for 3-4minutes with boiling water (212 degrees)
> **Herbals, Tisanes and Rooibos**—boiling water, Steep for 7 minutes.
> **Oolongs**—195 degree Water. Steep for 3 minutes.
> **Whites and Greens**—Steaming water—175 degrees. Steep for 3 minutes.

Over steeping any tea will make your tea bitter! Use a timer and get it right.  Using water that is too hot for whites and greens will also make your tea bitter!

### Got Milk?

Many tea drinkers are under the misconception that cream should be added to your tea, not milk. Actually cream and half-n-half are too heavy. Milk can be added to most black teas and to some oolongs. I don't recommend it for herbals, greens and whites.

The debate continues as to whether to pour milk into your cup before your tea or to add milk after you pour your tea. Really, the decision is yours! I always recommend tasting your tea first before adding milk or any sugar. You would be surprised how perfectly wonderful many teas are without any additions.

I think you're ready to start your tea adventure!

Until Our Next Pot of Tea,

Recipes From
The Traveling Tea Ladies
*–Viva Las Vegas*

## *Bluegrass Derby Pie*

"I'm worried about her, Amelia. Has she returned your phone calls lately?" Olivia asked as she took another sip of her tea and continued devouring the last few bites of bluegrass derby pie. "You've outdone yourself today, Lily. Would you box two of these pies to go? Lincoln will go ape over this dessert!" —Chapter One

> 1 cup light corn syrup
> 3/4 cup light brown sugar
> 4 tablespoons unsalted butter, melted
> 3 large eggs
> 2 tablespoons whiskey
> 1/4 teaspoon salt
> 2 cups pecan halves
> 1/2 cup semisweet chocolate chips
> 9 inch pie crust, unbaked

Preheat oven to 350° F. Whisk together corn syrup, brown sugar, butter, eggs, whiskey, and salt; fold in pecans and chocolate chips.

Pour mixture into the piecrust and bake until the center is set but still slightly wobbly, 40 to 50 minutes. Let cool before serving.

## Tennessee Pot Roast

"Don't be silly, Sarah. Get a pot of tea or share our pot of Jasmine. I'm in no hurry today. Shane's picking up Charlie from football and Emma is at choir practice. There's a roast in the oven, so I can take my time getting home."
—Chapter One

Marinade:
2 small onions quartered
1/3 cup olive oil
Crushed garlic
1/4 cup worcheshire sauce
1/2 cup Jack Daniels Tennessee Honey
2 – 3 lb. Prime cut chuck roast

Pour marinade over roast in 1 gallon freezer bag. Refrigerate for at least 1 hour or overnight. Dump entire contents of bag into a 5-quart Dutch oven or ovenproof pot with a tight-fitting lid. Preheat oven to 350 degrees.Cover; bake until roast is tender, 3 ½ to 4 hours. Transfer roast to a cutting board and thinly slice meat against the grain.

## *Lily's Cherry Cream Cheese Brownies*

"I haven't heard from Cassandra either. I was hoping you had. That's why I called you to meet me today. I want to respect her privacy, but I'm worried about her, Liv. She looked so thin the last time I saw her at the symphony showcase house," I recalled as I wiped the traces of cherry cream cheese brownie from the corners of my mouth.
—Chapter One

1 package (8 oz) cream cheese, softened

1/4 cup sugar

1/4 cup chopped well-drained maraschino cherries

1 teaspoon maraschino cherry juice

1 egg

1 box (1 lb 2 oz) Premium brownie mix with pouch of chocolate fudge included

1/3 cup vegetable oil

3/4 cup water

1 egg

Heat oven to 350°F (325°F for dark or nonstick pan). Grease bottom of 9-inch square pan with cooking spray or shortening.

In medium bowl, beat cream cheese, sugar, cherries, cherry juice and 1 egg with spoon; set aside.

In another medium bowl, combine brownie mix, pouch of chocolate fudge, oil, water and 1 egg until well blended. Spread half of the batter in pan. Spread cream cheese mixture over batter. Carefully spoon remaining batter on top; spread gently to cover.

Bake 43 to 47 minutes (51 to 55 minutes for dark pan) or until toothpick inserted 1 inch from side of pan comes out almost clean. Cool completely, about 1 ½ hours, before cutting. Store covered in refrigerator.

## *Italian Meatball Vegetable Soup*

"That sounds like a plan," Olivia agreed. I shook my head in amusement. Of course she would join Sarah for soup. Sarah walked over the counter and placed an order for two cups of the delicious soup laden with tomatoes, Italian green beans, kidney beans, and of course homemade mini meatballs. —Chapter One

2  8 oz. cans Italian diced tomatoes
   (Oregano & Basil seasoned)
2  8 oz. cans Italian green beans drained
2  8 oz. cans red kidney beans
1  large family size can concentrated tomato soup
1  chopped green pepper
1  small onion minced
2  cloves garlic minced
2  Tablespoons olive oil
2  Tablespoons Italian seasoning
Salt & Pepper to taste
Large package pre-cooked meatballs cut in half

Sauté olive oil, onion, garlic, and green pepper over low to medium heat until tender. Add remaining ingredients and increase heat to high. Add 2 cups water and bring to a boil. Reduce heat and simmer for 30 minutes or more. Add meatballs, Italian seasoning and salt & pepper to taste. Serve with favorite Italian bread.

## *Serendipity's Frozen Hot Chocolate*

**"Are you ready to take a lunch break? I've been dying to eat at Serendipity's and try their famous iced hot chocolate! You'd love it," I encouraged her.** —Chapter Five

6 pieces (½-ounce) chocolate , a variety of your favorites

2 teaspoons store-bought hot chocolate mix

1 ½ tablespoons sugar

1 ½ cups milk

3 cups ice

Whipped cream

Chocolate shavings

Chop the chocolate into small pieces. Place it in the top of a double boiler over simmering water. Stir occasionally until melted. Add the hot chocolate mix and sugar. Stir until completely melted. Remove from heat and slowly add ½ cup of milk until smooth. Cool to room temperature. In a blender, place the remaining cup of milk, the room-temperature chocolate mixture and the ice. Blend on high speed until smooth and the consistency of a frozen daiquiri. Pour into a giant goblet and top with whipped cream and chocolate shavings.

Get Serendipity 3's own chocolate mix at:
    www.serendipity3.com

## *Sour Cream Pound Cake*

"And there was a feast waiting for us when we reached our destination," Olivia continued. "There were buffalo burgers, steak fries, grilled corn with black beans, and the best sour cream pound cake with fresh fruit that I have ever eaten. It was wonderful!" —Chapter Six

    1 ½ cups butter, softened
    3 cups sugar
    6 large eggs
    3 cups all-purpose flour
    1/2 teaspoon salt
    1/4 teaspoon baking soda
    8-oz container sour cream
    1 teaspoon lemon extract
    1/4 teaspoon almond extract

Beat butter at medium speed with an electric mixer until creamy. Gradually add sugar, beating at medium speed until light and fluffy. Add eggs, 1 at a time, beating just until the yolk disappears.

Sift together flour, salt, and baking soda. Add to butter mixture alternately with sour cream, beginning and ending with flour mixture. Beat batter at low speed just until blended after each addition. Stir in extracts. Pour into a greased and floured 12-cup tube pan.

Bake at 325° for 1 hour and 20 minutes to 1 hour and 30 minutes or until a long wooden pick inserted in center of cake comes out clean. Cool in pan on a wire rack 10 minutes. Remove cake from pan, and cool completely on wire rack.

## *Godiva Chocolate Martini*

"Would anyone care to begin with a cocktail this evening?"
a petite blonde server graciously asked our table.
"I'm going to need one," I disclosed to Shane. "This could
be a long night. I'd like a chocolate martini," I told the
server. —Chapter Six

     1 ½ shots Godiva® chocolate liqueur
     1 ½ shots creme de cacao
     1/2 shot vodka
     2 ½ shots half-and-half

Mix all ingredients in a shaker with ice, shake and pour into
a chilled cocktail glass

# In-And-Out Lemontini

"Sarah, Lucy? Would you care for a cocktail? We're in Vegas
after all," Shane suggested.
"I'll have one of those 'in and out lemontinis,'" Lucy
spoke up.
"None for me," Sarah declined. "I want to be clear headed
tonight so I can remember every moment," she beamed.
—Chapter Six

    3 oz vodka
    splash of lemoncello
    lemon twist for garnish
    Preparation:
    Pour a splash of lemoncello into a frozen cocktail glass.
    Swirl the liqueur around in the glass until all surfaces
     are coated.
    Shake the vodka in a cocktail shaker filled with ice.
    Throw away any excess lemoncello in the glass.
    Strain the shake vodka into the coated cocktail glass.
    Garnish with a lemon twist.

## *Devils Handshake*

"I'll have a Devil's Handshake," Jonathan spoke up.
"That sounds delicious! What's in it?" Sarah questioned.
"It's sweet and sour with tequila, ginger puree, and a splash
 of pineapple juice. You should have one," he urged.

– Chapter Six

    1 ½ parts Tequila
    3/4 parts lime juice
    1/2 parts simple syrup
    1 part pineapple juice
    1 tsp sweet ginger puree*
    1/4 part egg white
    Garnish with lime wedge

Dry shake vigorously, ice and shake again.

Strain onto fresh ice in a highball glass.

Garnish with a lime wedge.

*To make your own ginger puree: Cut thin slices of fresh ginger and process in a food processor or blender until smooth. Optionally, add a teaspoon of sugar. Place the puree into an ice cube tray and freeze. Place the cubes in a bag or sealed container in the freezer until ready to make the drink. 1 cube makes about 2 tablespoons (depending on the size of the cube tray) and allow a few minutes to thaw.

# RESOURCE GUIDE

Here is a list of places to visit on the web or when you're in "Sin City!" I hope you'll have fun creating your own adventure with these wonderful sights.

**Bellagio Las Vegas**

    3600 S. Las Vegas Blvd. 89109

    www.Bellagio.com

    (423) 926-0123

    Featuring:

    Fiori Di Como

    Conservatory and Botanical Garden

    Jean Philippe Patisserie and Chocolate Fountain (www.jpchocolates.com)

    Fountains of Bellagio

**Olives by Chef Todd English**

    www.toddenglish.com

    (702) 693-8181

## Cirque du Soleil

www.CirqueduSoleil.com

## Picasso's Restaurant

At the Bellagio Las Vegas

(702) 693-8105

## Haunted Vegas Tour

www.HauntedVegasTours.com

(702) 677-6499

## The Forum Shops of Cesar's Palace

3570 S. Las Vegas Blvd.

www.CaesarsPalace.com

## World Tea Expo

www.World TeaExpo.com

## North American Tea Championship

www.TeaChampionship.com

## Serendipity's

3570 S. Las Vegas Blvd. 89109

www.caesarspalace.com/restaurants/

serendipity-3.html#.UYPBwcjD9D8

(702) 731-7373

**United States Parachute Association**
www.uspa.org

**Skeptic's Magazine**
www.Skeptic.com

**Gondola ride Venetian hotel**
3355 S. Las Vegas Blvd. 89109
www.Venetian.com
(702) 414-1000

**Carnevino, Palazzo of Venetian hotel** (Mario batali)
3325 S. Las Vegas Blvd. 89109
www.Carnevino.com
(702) 789-4141

**Cocolini's Gelatos**
3355 S. Las Vegas Blvd 89109

**Thunder From Down Under**
www.thunderfromdownunder.com
(702) 732-8927

**Excalibur Hotel**
3850 S. Las Vegas Blvd. 89109

# About the Author

Former tea room owner, Melanie O'Hara, is a graduate of Southern Methodist University and East Tennessee State University. Her love of tea was ignited after a semester abroad studying international communications in London, England.

She shares her passion with people inspired to follow their tea dreams through her Tea Academy classes and tea tours.

Melanie, her husband Keith and their brood of children make their home in East Tennessee. When she is not writing, conducting a tea lecture, giving a cooking with tea demonstration or leading a tea tour, you can find her at the helm of her online business, Smoky Mountain Coffee, Herb & Tea Company.

For more information about The Tea Academy, booking your own tea tour, or attending a tea class, e-mail Melanie:

Melanie@TheTravelingTeaLadies.com

And join her tea adventure on Facebook where the tea party never ends!

# THE TEA ACADEMY

Consulting & Training for Tea Professionals

www.TheTeaAcademy.com

www.SmokyMountainCoffee-Herb-Tea.com

Official Tea Company of *The Traveling Tea Ladies*

## LYONS
## LEGACY
### PUBLISHING™

Traveling Tea Ladies readers, for other Lyons Legacy titles
you may enjoy, or to purchase other books in The Traveling
Tea Ladies Series, signed by the author, visit our website:

www.LyonsLegacyPublishing.com

Love the teas and coffees described in this book?
Would you like to purchase more books in the series?
Shop with us online!

www.TheTravelingTeaLadies.com

# theTraveling
# Tea Ladies™

Gourmet Teas, Organic Coffees,
Autographed Books, Gift Baskets & Apparel

Follow Us On Facebook

# Savannah Skies
## *Return to Tybee Island*

Set in the marshlands of coastal Georgia, *Savannah Skies Return to Tybee Island* shares the deeply moving story of one woman's courage as she navigates heartache, tragedy, healing, and forgiveness.

Savannah Brennan Scott is an accomplished New York book editor secretly fighting to keep her marriage to her philandering husband intact. When Savannah returns home for a family wedding on Tybee Island without her husband Derek, she knows tongues are sure to wag among her large Irish family. She struggles to be true to herself and risk disappointing her overbearing and excessively critical mother who never approved of "that damn Yankee." Savannah is forced to announce her pending divorce at her cousin's rehearsal dinner after Derek shows up declaring his intentions to marry his pregnant lover. Facing an uncertain future and letting go of the past she discovers the healing you can only find back home. You'll laugh, you'll cry and you'll fall in love with Melanie O'Hara's newest heroine. *Savannah Skies Return to Tybee Island* will be released fall 2013.

CPSIA information can be obtained at www.ICGtesting.com
Printed in the USA
LVOW05s0051141114

413636LV00003B/61/P